YOUR PERSONAL
HOROSCOPE
2007

SCORPIO

YOUR PERSONAL HOROSCOPE 2007

SCORPIO

24th October–22nd November

igloo

igloo

This edition published by Igloo Books Ltd,
Garrard Way, Kettering, NN16 8TD
www.igloo-books.com
E-mail: Info@igloo-books.com

Produced for Igloo Books by W. Foulsham & Co. Ltd,
The Publishing House, Bennetts Close, Cippenham,
Slough, Berkshire SL1 5AP, England

ISBN 13: 978-1-84561-354-9
ISBN 10: 1-84561-354-6

Printed in China

CONTENTS

INTRODUCTION

Your Personal Horoscopes have been specifically created to allow you to get the most from astrological patterns and the way they have a bearing on not only your zodiac sign, but nuances within it. Using the diary section of the book you can read about the influences and possibilities of each and every day of the year. It will be possible for you to see when you are likely to be cheerful and happy or those times when your nature is in retreat and you will be more circumspect. The diary will help to give you a feel for the specific 'cycles' of astrology and the way they can subtly change your day-to-day life. For example, when you see the sign ☿, this means that the planet Mercury is retrograde at that time. Retrograde means it appears to be running backwards through the zodiac. Such a happening has a significant effect on communication skills, but this is only one small aspect of how the Personal Horoscope can help you.

With Your Personal Horoscope the story doesn't end with the diary pages. It includes simple ways for you to work out the zodiac sign the Moon occupied at the time of your birth, and what this means for your personality. In addition, if you know the time of day you were born, it is possible to discover your Ascendant, yet another important guide to your personal make-up and potential.

Many readers are interested in relationships and in knowing how well they get on with people of other astrological signs. You might also be interested in the way you appear to very different sorts of individuals. If you are such a person, the section on Venus will be of particular interest. Despite the rapidly changing position of this planet, you can work out your Venus sign, and learn what bearing it will have on your life.

Using Your Personal Horoscope you can travel on one of the most fascinating and rewarding journeys that anyone can take – the journey to a better realisation of self.

THE ESSENCE OF SCORPIO

Exploring the Personality of Scorpio the Scorpion

(24TH OCTOBER – 22ND NOVEMBER)

What's in a sign?

To say that you are a little complicated and somewhat difficult to understand is probably a great understatement. The basic reason for this lies in the peculiar nature of Scorpio rulership. In terms of the elements, your zodiac sign is a Water sign. This makes you naturally emotional, deep, somewhat reserved and ever anxious to help those around you. As a direct contrast, classical astrologers always maintained that your planetary ruler was Mars. Mars is the planet of combat and aggression, being positive and dominant under most circumstances. So it can be judged from the start that there are great contradictions within the basic Scorpio nature.

It's a fact that many people are naturally cautious of Scorpio people. Perhaps this isn't surprising. Under most circumstances you appear to be quiet and peaceful, but the situation is a little like a smoking bomb. When it comes to defending yourself, or in particular those people who you see as being important to you, there is virtually no limit to which you would refuse to go. Generally speaking our ancient ancestors were extremely wise in terms of the names they gave to the different zodiac signs. Consider the apparently diminutive and retiring scorpion. It doesn't go looking for trouble and is generally happy to remain in the shadows. However, if it is provoked, or even attacked, it will take on adversaries many times its own size. It carries a barbed sting in its tail and will strike without any additional warning if necessary.

All the same, the Scorpio reputation may be a little undeserved. Yours is one of the most compassionate and caring of all the zodiac signs. When it comes to working on behalf of humanity, especially the oppressed, the sick or the disenfranchised, you show your true mettle. You cannot stand the thought of people suffering unjustifiably, which is why many of the great social reformers and even freedom fighters had the same zodiac sign as you do.

As a Scorpio you are likely to be intuitive (some would say psychic) and under most circumstances you are more than willing to follow that little voice inside yourself that tells you how to behave in any given situation.

Scorpio resources

Your nature is so very often understated that it might be said that your greatest resource is surprise. You have the ability to shock people constantly, even those who think they understand you perfectly well. This brings us back to the creature for which your zodiac sign is named. A scorpion is diminutive – and would represent a tasty snack for any would-be predator. However, it defies logic by standing its ground and fighting back. When it does, woe betide the aggressor that refuses to take account of its presence. And so it is with you. Quiet, even reserved, you tend to get on with your work. This you do efficiently and without undue fuss, approaching each task with the same methodical attitude. People often don't even realise that you are around. And then, when they least expect it, there you are!

The ability to surprise means that you often get on in life against heavy odds. In addition you have great resilience and fortitude. It is possible for you to continue to work long and hard under circumstances that would force others to retreat. Most Scorpio people would not consider themselves to be tough – in fact quite a few are positively neurotic when it comes to matters associated with their own health. Yet you can endure hardship well and almost always win through in the end.

It's true that you may not be quite as confident as you could be. If you were, people would notice you more and that would detract from that all-important element of surprise that makes you so formidable, and which is definitely the most important weapon in your armoury. However, it is clear that your greatest resource is compassion, and on those occasions when you really allow it to show, you display yourself as being one of the most important allies to your fellow men and women.

At a practical level you are more than capable and can often be expected to perform tasks that you haven't necessarily undertaken before. You have a deep intelligence and good powers to reason things out. Most important of all is a determination that no other zodiac sign can match.

Beneath the surface

This section of an account of the typical Scorpio nature could fill an entire book in itself because you are such a complicated person. However, there are certain advantages to being a Scorpio. For example, nobody is going to run away with the idea that you are basically uncomplicated and shallow. It ought to be clear enough to the dullest observer that there is a boiling, seething volcano bubbling away beneath the surface of almost every Scorpio subject.

You are often accused of having a slightly dark view of life, and it's true that many Scorpio people enjoy a rather morbid curiosity and are fascinated by subjects that make other people shudder. At the same time you could hardly be described as being one of life's natural optimists. Part of the reason for this lies in the fact that you have been disappointed in the past and may have arrived at the conclusion that to expect the worst is often the most sensible course of action. At least that way you are likely to mitigate some of the potential depression regarding failures in the future.

Although this way of thinking is somewhat faulty, it comes so naturally to the Scorpio subject that it actually works very well, though it has to be said that it might be responsible for a tendency to hold back on occasions.

Assessing the way your inner mind works is as difficult for you as it is for any outsider. Even individuals who have been friends for years will sometimes come desperately unstuck if they arrive at the conclusion that they know well what makes you tick. In the recesses of your mind you are passionate, driving, restless, dissatisfied and frequently disappointed with your own efforts. On the other hand, you have the power to make dreams into realities and are excellent at hatching plans that will benefit people far from your own circle and circumstances. Being a tireless worker on behalf of the oppressed, the fate of humanity as a whole is ever an inner concern.

When you love you do so with great width and depth. Your capacity for jealousy knows no bounds and there are times when you can be as destructive to yourself as you ever could be regarding any other individual. Yet for all this your inner mind is lofty and can soar like an eagle on occasions. If the world at large was able to fathom just one tenth of the way your inner mind actually works, people would find you even more fascinating than they do already. But perhaps it's best that they don't. The deepest recesses of Scorpio are an intense secret and will usually stay that way.

Making the best of yourself

It isn't hard to find a single word that describes the way you can make the best of yourself, especially when viewed by the world at large. That word is 'communication'. When difficulties arise in your life, especially concerning other people, it's usually because you haven't managed to get your message across, and probably because you haven't even tried to do so. There is much to your nature that is electric, powerful and magnetic. These qualities make you potentially popular and fascinating to a wealth of individuals. Hide these qualities beneath too brusque an exterior and you can seem dark and brooding.

Of course it's a fine line and one that isn't easy to walk. You are constantly worried that if you show people what really makes you tick, they will not find you interesting at all. In reality this concern is totally without foundation. There is more than enough depth about you to last several lifetimes. It doesn't matter how much you give of yourself to the world at large, there are always going to be surprises galore to follow.

Use the dynamic qualities of your nature to the full. Traditionally your ruling planet is Mars – a real go-getter of a planetary ruler and one that imbues you with tremendous power to get things done at a practical level. On the way you need to show how much you care about others. Amidst a plethora of gifts offered to you by the celestial spheres, your ability to help others is likely to be top of the list. When you are giving you are also usually approachable. For you the two go hand in hand. Avoid allowing yourself to become morose or inward looking and always strive to find simple answers to simple questions.

Stick to some sort of work that you find interesting. That can be almost anything to a Scorpio, as long as it feeds the inner you. It does need to carry a degree of diversity and should ideally have an end product that is easy to see. On your journey through life don't get carried away with daydreams – yet on the other hand avoid losing your great potential to make them come true.

The impressions you give

This is one area of your life over which you do have a great deal of control. If the adage 'what you see is what you get' turns out to be true for many signs of the zodiac, it certainly isn't the case with you. The complexity of your nature makes it difficult for even you to find 'the real Scorpio', and in any case this tends to change from day to day. However, regarding some matters there isn't any doubt at all. Firstly you are deeply magnetic and possess the ability to arouse an instinctive fascination in others. Ally this to your propensity for being very positive in your decision making and you have a potentially formidable combination.

Most people already think of you as being an extremely interesting person. Unfortunately they may also occasionally consider you to be a little cool and somewhat difficult to approach. Neither of these impressions are true, it's simply that you are quite shy at heart, and sometimes find it difficult to believe that you could be liked by certain individuals. Learn to throw this erroneous assumption out of the window, and instead, expect to be viewed positively. To do so would make all the difference and would clear the way so that your more personable side can show all the time.

Very few people who know you well could fail to realise that you care deeply, especially about the well-being of the oppressed. You have a truly noble spirit, a fact that shines through in practically everything you do – yet another reason to be noticed.

It's true that you can sometimes make your secretive quality into an art form, which those looking in from the outside might find rather difficult to deal with. This represents another outward aspect of your nature that could so easily be altered. By all means keep your secrets, though not about matters that are of no real note whatsoever. In a single phrase, try to lighten up a little. It's all you need to be almost perfect!

The way forward

It must first be held in mind that Scorpio people are complicated. That's something you simply cannot get away from, no matter how much you might try. On the one hand you can deal with practical matters almost instinctively. You are resourceful, deep thinking, intense and fascinating. On the other side of the coin you are often too fond of luxury and will frequently withdraw yourself from situations that you do not care to pursue. You can be quite stubborn and can even bear a grudge if you feel that you have been provoked. It is suggested in astrology that no quality of nature is necessarily good or bad, it really depends on the way it is used. For example, stubbornness can be considered a terrible fault, but not if you were being awkward concerning the obvious rights of an oppressed person or group. It turns out that Scorpio has more of a potential to be 'saint or sinner' than any zodiac sign. As long as you examine your motives in any given situation, whilst at the same time trying to cultivate a degree of flexibility that is not one of your natural gifts, then you won't go far wrong.

Turn on the charm when it is necessary because it will rarely if ever let you down. Think about the way you can serve the world, but don't preach about it. Love sincerely, but don't allow jealousy to spoil things. Be constructive in your determination and don't get on your high horse when it isn't necessary. Follow these simple rules for the best chance of progress.

Of course there are many positives around to start with. You are a very loyal friend, are capable of being extremely brave and tend to be very committed to family members. At the same time you are trustworthy and can work long and hard using your own initiative. Although you sometimes worry about your health, you are more robust than most and can endure a high degree of hardship if necessary. You don't take kindly to criticism but can be flexible enough to accept it if you know it is intended for your own good.

Few people doubt your sincerity – that is, when they know what you believe. So it's important to lay your thoughts on the line right from the start. And even if you don't choose to treat the whole world as a friend, you are capable of gathering a little circle around you who would never let you down. Do make sure, however, that this 'inner group' isn't simply comprised of other Scorpios!

SCORPIO ON THE CUSP

Astrological profiles are altered for those people born at either the beginning or the end of a zodiac sign, or, more properly, on the cusps of a sign. In the case of Scorpio this would be on the 24th of October and for two or three days after, and similarly at the end of the sign, probably from the 20th to the 22nd of November.

The Libra Cusp – October 24th to 26th

You are probably generally considered to be a bright and breezy sort of character, with a great deal of enthusiasm for life. Despite this, few people would doubt that you are a shrewd operator, and that you know what you want and have a fairly good idea of how to go about getting it. Not everyone likes you as much as you would wish, but that's because the Libran side of your nature longs for popularity, while set against this is your deep Scorpio need to speak your mind, even when you know that other people might wish you did not indulge in this trait very frequently.

In love, you typify the split between these two signs. On the one hand you are passionate, sincere and intense, while on the other your Libran responses can cause a certain fickle sort of affection to show sometimes, probably to the confusion of those with whom you are involved at a personal level. Nevertheless, few people would find fault with your basic nature and there isn't much doubt that your heart is in the right place.

When it comes to career matters, you have a very fortunate combination. Scorpio can sometimes be accused of lacking diplomacy, but nothing could be further from the truth with Libra. As a result, you have what it takes in terms of determination but at the same time you are capable of seeing the point of view put forward by colleagues. You tend to rise to the top of the tree and, with your mixture of raw ability and humour that most of the world approves of, you can stay there.

You won't be the sort of person to make quite as many enemies as Scorpio taken alone might do, and you need the cut and thrust of the world much more than the retiring creature after whom your zodiac sign is named. Try not to be controversial and do your best to retain a sense of humour, which is essential to your well-being. Few would doubt the fact that your heart is in the right place and your creative potential could be second to none. Most important of all, you need the self-satisfaction that comes from living in the real world.

The Sagittarius Cusp – November 20th to 22nd

You can be a really zany character, with a love of life that is second to none. Add to this a penetrating insight, a razor-sharp wit and an instinctive intuition that is quite remarkable and we find in you a formidable person. It's true that not everyone understands what makes you tick, probably least of all yourself, but you strive to be liked and really do want to advertise your willingness to learn and to grow, which isn't always the province of Scorpio when taken alone. Your capacity for work knows no bounds, though you don't really like to get your hands dirty and would feel more content when telling others what to do.

In a career sense, you need to be in a position from which you are able to delegate. This is not because you are afraid of hard work yourself, far from it, but you possess a strong ability to see through problems and you are a natural director of others. Sales careers may interest you, or a position from which you can organise and arrange things. However, you hate to be tied down to one place for long, so you would be at your best when allowed to move around freely and do things in your own way.

You are a natural social reformer, mainly because you are sure that you know what is right and just. In the main you are correct in your assumptions, but there are occasions when you should realise that there is more than one form of truth. Perhaps you are not always quite as patient with certain individuals as you might be but these generally tend to be people who show traits of cruelty or cunning. As a family person, you care very much for the people who figure most prominently in your life. Sometimes you are a definite home bird, with a preference for what you know and love, but this is offset by a restless trend within your nature that often sends you off into the wide blue yonder, chasing rainbows that the Scorpio side of your nature doubts are even there. Few would doubt your charm, your magnetism, or your desire to get ahead in life in almost any way possible. You combine patience with genuine talent and make a loyal, interesting and entertaining friend or lover.

SCORPIO AND ITS ASCENDANTS

The nature of every individual on the planet is composed of the rich variety of zodiac signs and planetary positions that were present at the time of their birth. Your Sun sign, which in your case is Scorpio, is one of the many factors when it comes to assessing the unique person you are. Probably the most important consideration, other than your Sun sign, is to establish the zodiac sign that was rising over the eastern horizon at the time that you were born. This is your Ascending or Rising sign. Most popular astrology fails to take account of the Ascendant, and yet its importance remains with you from the very moment of your birth, through every day of your life. The Ascendant is evident in the way you approach the world, and so, when meeting a person for the first time, it is this astrological influence that you are most likely to notice first. Our Ascending sign essentially represents what we appear to be, while the Sun sign is what we feel inside ourselves.

The Ascendant also has the potential for modifying our overall nature. For example, if you were born at a time of day when Scorpio was passing over the eastern horizon (this would be around the time of dawn) then you would be classed as a double Scorpio. As such, you would typify this zodiac sign, both internally and in your dealings with others. However, if your Ascendant sign turned out to be a Fire sign, such as Aries, there would be a profound alteration of nature, away from the expected qualities of Scorpio.

One of the reasons why popular astrology often ignores the Ascendant is that it has always been rather difficult to establish. We have found a way to make this possible by devising an easy-to-use table, which you will find on page 157 of this book. Using this, you can establish your Ascendant sign at a glance. You will need to know your rough time of birth, then it is simply a case of following the instructions.

For those readers who have no idea of their time of birth it might be worth allowing a good friend, or perhaps your partner, to read through the section that follows this introduction. Someone who deals with you on a regular basis may easily discover your Ascending sign, even though you could have some difficulty establishing it for yourself. A good understanding of this component of your nature is essential if you want to be aware of that 'other person' who is responsible for the way you make contact with the world at large. Your Sun sign, Ascendant sign, and the other pointers in this book will, together, allow you a far better understanding of what makes you tick as an individual. Peeling back the different layers of your astrological make-up can be an enlightening experience, and the Ascendant may represent one of the most important layers of all.

Scorpio with Scorpio Ascendant

This is one of the most potent of all astrological possibilities, but how it is used depends so very much on the individual who possesses it. On the one hand you are magnetic, alluring, sexy, deep and very attractive, whilst at the same time you are capable of being stubborn, self-seeking, vain, over-sensitive and fathomless. It has to be said that under most circumstances the first set of adjectives are the most appropriate, and that is because you keep control of the deeper side, refusing to allow it absolute control over your conscious life. You are able to get almost anything you want from life, but first you have to discover what that might be. The most important factor of all, however, is the way you can offer yourself, totally and without reservation to a needy world.

Self-sacrifice is a marvellous thing, but you can go too far on occasions. The furthest extreme for Scorpios here is a life that is totally dedicated to work and prayer. For the few this is admirable, for the still earth-based, less so. Finding a compromise is not easy as you are not always in touch with yourself. Feed the spiritual, curb the excesses, accept the need for luxury, and be happy.

Scorpio with Sagittarius Ascendant

There are many gains with this combination, and most of you reading this will already be familiar with the majority of them. Sagittarius offers a bright and hopeful approach to life, but may not always have the staying power and the patience to get what it really needs. Scorpio, on the other hand, can be too deep for its own good, is very self-seeking on occasions and extremely giving to others. Both the signs have problems when taken on their own, and, it has to be said, double the difficulties when they come together. But this is not usually the case. Invariably the presence of Scorpio slows down the over-quick responses of the Archer, whilst the inclusion of Sagittarius prevents Scorpio from taking itself too seriously.

Life is so often a game of extremes, when all the great spiritual masters of humanity have indicated that a 'middle way' is the path to choose. You have just the right combination of skills and mental faculties to find that elusive path, and can bring great joy to yourself and others as a result. Most of the time you are happy, optimistic, helpful and a joy to know. You have mental agility, backed up by a stunning intuition, which itself would rarely let you down. Keep a sense of proportion and understand that your depth of intellect is necessary to curb your flighty side.

Scorpio with Capricorn Ascendant

If patience, perseverance and a solid ability to get where you want to go are considered to be the chief components of a happy life, then you should be skipping about every day. Unfortunately this is not always the case and here we have two zodiac signs, both of which can be too deep for their own good. Both Scorpio and Capricorn are inclined to take themselves rather too seriously and your main lesson in life, and some would say the reason you have adopted this zodiac combination, is to 'lighten up'. If all that determination is pushed in the direction of your service to the world at large, you are seen as being one of the kindest people imaginable. This is really the only option for you, because if you turn this tremendous potential power inwards all the time you will become brooding, secretive and sometimes even selfish. Your eyes should be turned towards a needy humanity, which can be served with the dry but definite wit of Capricorn and the true compassion of Scorpio.

It is impossible with this combination to indicate what areas of life suit you the best. Certainly you adore luxury in all its forms, and yet you can get by with almost nothing. You desire travel, and at the same time love the comforts and stability of home. The people who know you best are aware that you are rather special. Listen to what they say.

Scorpio with Aquarius Ascendant

Here we have a combination that shows much promise and a flexibility that allows many changes in direction, allied to a power to succeed, sometimes very much against all the odds. Aquarius lightens the load of the Scorpio mind, turning the depths into potential and making intuitive foresight into a means for getting on in life. There are depths here, because even airy Aquarius isn't too easy to understand, and it is therefore a fact that some people with this combination will always be something of a mystery. However, even this fact can be turned to your advantage because it means that people will always be looking at you. Confidence is so often the key to success in life and the Scorpio–Aquarius mix offers this, or at least appears to do so. Even when this is not entirely the case, the fact that everyone around you believes it to be true is often enough.

You are usually good to know, and show a keen intellect and a deep intelligence, aided by a fascination for life that knows no bounds. When at your best you are giving, understanding, balanced and active. On those occasions when things are not going well for you, beware a stubborn streak and the need to be sensational. Keep it light and happy and you won't go far wrong. Most of you are very, very well loved.

Scorpio with Pisces Ascendant

You stand a chance of disappearing so deep into yourself that other people would need one of those long ladders that cave explorers use, just to find you. It isn't really your fault because both Scorpio and Pisces are Water signs, which are difficult to understand, and you have them both. But that doesn't mean that you should be content to remain in the dark, and the warmth of your nature is all you need to shine a light on the wonderful qualities you possess. But the primary word of warning is that you must put yourself on display and allow others to know what you are, before their appreciation of these facts becomes apparent.

As a server of the world you are second to none and it is hard to find a person with this combination who is not, in some way, looking out for the people around them. Immensely attractive to others, you are also one of the most sought-after lovers. Much of this has to do with your deep and abiding charm, but the air of mystery that surrounds you also helps. Some of you will marry too early, and end up regretting the fact, though the majority of people with Scorpio and Pisces will find the love they deserve in the end. You are able, just, firm but fair, though a sucker for a hard luck story and as kind as the day is long. It's hard to imagine how so many good points could be ignored by others.

Scorpio with Aries Ascendant

The two very different faces of Mars come together in this potent, magnetic and quite awe-inspiring combination. Your natural inclination is towards secrecy, and this fact, together with the natural attractions of the sensual Scorpio nature, makes you the object of great curiosity. This means that you will not go short of attention and should ensure that you are always being analysed by people who may never get to know you at all. At heart you prefer your own company, and yet life appears to find means to push you into the public gaze time and again. Most people with this combination ooze sex appeal and can use this fact as a stepping stone to personal success, yet without losing any integrity or loosening the cords of a deeply moralistic nature.

On those occasions when you do lose your temper, there isn't a character in the length and breadth of the zodiac who would have either the words or the courage to stand against the stream of invective that follows. On really rare occasions you might even scare yourself. A simple look is enough to show family members when you are not amused. Few people are left unmoved by your presence in their life.

Scorpio with Taurus Ascendant

The first, last and most important piece of advice for you is not to take yourself, or anyone else, too seriously. This might be rather a tall order because Scorpio intensifies the deeper qualities of Taurus and can make you rather lacking in the sense of humour that we all need to live our lives in this most imperfect of worlds. You are naturally sensual by nature. This shows itself in a host of ways. In all probability you can spend hours in the bath, love to treat yourself to good food and drink and take your greatest pleasure in neat and orderly surroundings. This can often alienate you from those who live in the same house because other people need to use the bathroom from time to time and they cannot remain tidy indefinitely.

You tend to worry a great deal about things which are really not too important, but don't take this statement too seriously or you will begin to worry about this fact too! You often need to lighten up and should always do your best to tell yourself that most things are not half so important as they seem to be. Be careful over the selection of a life partner and if possible choose someone who is naturally funny and who does not take life anywhere near as seriously as you are inclined to do. At work you are more than capable and in all probability everyone relies heavily on your wise judgements.

Scorpio with Gemini Ascendant

What you are and what you appear to be can be two entirely different things with this combination. Although you appear to be every bit as chatty and even as flighty as Gemini tends to be, nothing could be further from the truth. In reality you have many deep and penetrating insights, all of which are geared towards sorting out potential problems before they come along. Few people would have the ability to pull the wool over your eyes, and you show a much more astute face to the world than is often the case for Gemini taken on its own. The level of your confidence, although not earth-shattering, is much greater with this combination, and you would not be thwarted once you had made up your mind.

There is a slight danger here, however, because Gemini is always inclined to nerve problems of one sort or another. In the main these are slight and fleeting, though the presence of Scorpio can intensify reactions and heighten the possibility of depression, which would not be at all fortunate. The best way round this potential problem is to have a wealth of friends, plenty to do and the sort of variety in your life that suits your Mercury ruler. Financial success is not too difficult to achieve because you can easily earn money and then manage to hold on to it.

Scorpio with Cancer Ascendant

There are few more endearing zodiac combinations than this one. Both signs are Watery in nature and show a desire to work on behalf of humanity as a whole. The world sees you as being genuinely caring, full of sympathy for anyone in trouble and always ready to lend a hand when it is needed. You are a loyal friend, a great supporter of the oppressed and a lover of home and family. In a work sense you are capable, and command respect from your colleagues, even though this comes about courtesy of your quiet competence and not as a result of anything that you might happen to say.

But we should not get too carried away with external factors, or the way that others see you. Inside you are a boiling pool of emotion. You feel more strongly, love more deeply and hurt more fully than any other combination of the Water signs. Even those who think they know you really well would get a shock if they could take a stroll around the deeper recesses of your mind. Although these facts are true, they may be rather beside the point because it is a fact that the truth of your passion, commitment and deep convictions may only surface fully half a dozen times in your life. The fact is that you are a very private person at heart and you don't know how to be any other way.

Scorpio with Leo Ascendant

A Leo with intensity, that's what you are. You are mad about good causes and would argue the hind leg off a donkey in defence of your many ideals. If you are not out there saving the planet you could just be at home in the bath, thinking up the next way to save humanity from its own worst excesses. In your own life, although you love little luxuries, you are sparing and frugal, yet generous as can be to those you take to. It's a fact that you don't like everyone, and of course the same is true in reverse. It might be easier for you to understand why you can dislike than to appreciate the reverse side of the coin, for your pride can be badly dented on occasions. Scorpio brings a tendency to have down spells, though the fact that Leo is also strongly represented in your nature should prevent them from becoming a regular part of your life.

It is important for you to learn how to forgive and forget, and there isn't much point in bearing a grudge because you are basically too noble to do so. If something goes wrong, kiss the situation goodbye and get on with the next interesting adventure, of which there are many in your life. Stop–start situations sometimes get in the way, but there are plenty of people around who would be only too willing to lend a helping hand.

Scorpio with Virgo Ascendant

This is intensity carried through to the absolute. If you have a problem, it is that you fail to externalise all that is going on inside that deep, bubbling cauldron that is your inner self. Realising what you are capable of is not a problem; these only start when you have to make it plain to those around you what you want. Part of the reason for this is that you don't always understand yourself. You love intensely and would do absolutely anything for a person you are fond of, even though you might have to inconvenience yourself a great deal on the way. Relationships can cause you slight problems however, since you need to associate with people who at least come somewhere near to understanding what makes you tick. If you manage to bridge the gap between yourself and the world that constantly knocks on your door, you show yourself to be powerful, magnetic and compulsive.

There are times when you definitely prefer to stay quiet, though you do have a powerful ability to get your message across when you think it is necessary to do so. There are people around who might think that you are a push-over but they could easily get a shock when you sense that the time is right to answer back. You probably have a very orderly house and don't care for clutter of any sort.

Scorpio with Libra Ascendant

There is some tendency for you to be far more deep than the average Libran would appear to be and for this reason it is crucial that you lighten up from time to time. Every person with a Scorpio quality needs to remember that there is a happy and carefree side to all events and your Libran quality should allow you to bear this in mind. Sometimes you try to do too many things at the same time. This is fine if you take the casual overview of Libra, but less sensible when you insist on picking the last bone out of every potential, as is much more the case for Scorpio.

When worries come along, as they sometimes will, be able to listen to what your friends have to say and also realise that they are more than willing to work on your behalf, if only because you are so loyal to them. You do have a quality of self-deception, but this should not get in the way too much if you combine the instinctive actions of Libra with the deep intuition of your Scorpio component.

Probably the most important factor of this combination is your ability to succeed in a financial sense. You make a good manager, but not of the authoritarian sort. Jobs in the media or where you are expected to make up your mind quickly would suit you, because there is always an underpinning of practical sense that rarely lets you down.

THE MOON AND THE PART IT PLAYS IN YOUR LIFE

In astrology the Moon is probably the single most important heavenly body after the Sun. Its unique position, as partner to the Earth on its journey around the solar system, means that the Moon appears to pass through the signs of the zodiac extremely quickly. The zodiac position of the Moon at the time of your birth plays a great part in personal character and is especially significant in the build-up of your emotional nature.

Your Own Moon Sign

Discovering the position of the Moon at the time of your birth has always been notoriously difficult because tracking the complex zodiac positions of the Moon is not easy. This process has been reduced to three simple stages with our Lunar Tables. A breakdown of the Moon's zodiac positions can be found from page 35 onwards, so that once you know what your Moon Sign is, you can see what part this plays in the overall build-up of your personal character.

If you follow the instructions on the next page you will soon be able to work out exactly what zodiac sign the Moon occupied on the day that you were born and you can then go on to compare the reading for this position with those of your Sun sign and your Ascendant. It is partly the comparison between these three important positions that goes towards making you the unique individual you are.

HOW TO DISCOVER YOUR MOON SIGN

This is a three-stage process. You may need a pen and a piece of paper but if you follow the instructions below the process should only take a minute or so.

STAGE 1 First of all you need to know the Moon Age at the time of your birth. If you look at Moon Table 1, on page 33, you will find all the years between 1909 and 2007 down the left side. Find the year of your birth and then trace across to the right to the month of your birth. Where the two intersect you will find a number. This is the date of the New Moon in the month that you were born. You now need to count forward the number of days between the New Moon and your own birthday. For example, if the New Moon in the month of your birth was shown as being the 6th and you were born on the 20th, your Moon Age Day would be 14. If the New Moon in the month of your birth came after your birthday, you need to count forward from the New Moon in the previous month. If you were born in a Leap Year, remember to count the 29th February. You can tell if your birth year was a Leap Year if the last two digits can be divided by four. Whatever the result, jot this number down so that you do not forget it.

STAGE 2 Take a look at Moon Table 2 on page 34. Down the left hand column look for the date of your birth. Now trace across to the month of your birth. Where the two meet you will find a letter. Copy this letter down alongside your Moon Age Day.

STAGE 3 Moon Table 3 on page 34 will supply you with the zodiac sign the Moon occupied on the day of your birth. Look for your Moon Age Day down the left hand column and then for the letter you found in Stage 2. Where the two converge you will find a zodiac sign and this is the sign occupied by the Moon on the day that you were born.

Your Zodiac Moon Sign Explained

You will find a profile of all zodiac Moon Signs on pages 35 to 38, showing in yet another way how astrology helps to make you into the individual that you are. In each daily entry of the Astral Diary you can find the zodiac position of the Moon for every day of the year. This also allows you to discover your lunar birthdays. Since the Moon passes through all the signs of the zodiac in about a month, you can expect something like twelve lunar birthdays each year. At these times you are likely to be emotionally steady and able to make the sort of decisions that have real, lasting value.

MOON TABLE 1

YEAR	SEP	OCT	NOV	YEAR	SEP	OCT	NOV	YEAR	SEP	OCT	NOV
1909	14	14	13	1942	10	10	8	1975	5	5	3
1910	3	2	1	1943	29	29	27	1976	23	23	21
1911	22	21	20	1944	17	17	15	1977	13	12	11
1912	12	11	9	1945	6	6	4	1978	2	2/31	30
1913	30	29	28	1946	25	24	23	1979	21	20	19
1914	19	19	17	1947	14	14	12	1980	10	9	8
1915	9	8	7	1948	3	2	1	1981	28	27	26
1916	27	27	26	1949	23	21	20	1982	17	17	15
1917	15	15	14	1950	12	11	9	1983	7	6	4
1918	4	4	3	1951	1	1/30	29	1984	25	24	22
1919	23	23	22	1952	19	18	17	1985	14	14	12
1920	12	12	10	1953	8	8	6	1986	4	3	2
1921	2	1/30	29	1954	27	26	25	1987	23	22	21
1922	21	20	19	1955	16	15	14	1988	11	10	9
1923	10	10	8	1956	4	4	2	1989	29	29	28
1924	28	28	26	1957	23	23	21	1990	19	18	17
1925	18	17	16	1958	13	12	11	1991	8	8	6
1926	7	6	5	1959	3	2/31	30	1992	26	25	24
1927	25	25	24	1960	21	20	19	1993	16	15	14
1928	14	14	12	1961	10	9	8	1994	5	5	3
1929	3	2	1	1962	28	28	27	1995	24	24	22
1930	22	20	19	1963	17	17	15	1996	13	11	10
1931	12	11	9	1964	6	5	4	1997	2	2/31	30
1932	30	29	27	1965	25	24	22	1998	20	20	19
1933	19	19	17	1966	14	14	12	1999	9	9	8
1934	9	8	7	1967	4	3	2	2000	27	27	26
1935	27	27	26	1968	23	22	21	2001	17	17	16
1936	15	15	14	1969	11	10	9	2002	6	6	4
1937	4	4	3	1970	1	1/30	29	2003	26	25	24
1938	23	23	22	1971	19	19	18	2004	13	12	11
1939	13	12	11	1972	8	8	6	2005	3	2	1
1940	2	1/30	29	1973	27	26	25	2006	22	21	20
1941	21	20	19	1974	16	15	14	2007	12	11	9

TABLE 2

DAY	OCT	NOV
1	a	e
2	a	e
3	a	e
4	b	f
5	b	f
6	b	f
7	b	f
8	b	f
9	b	f
10	b	f
11	b	f
12	b	f
13	b	g
14	d	g
15	d	g
16	d	g
17	d	g
18	d	g
19	d	g
20	d	g
21	d	g
22	d	g
23	d	i
24	e	i
25	e	i
26	e	i
27	e	i
28	e	i
29	e	i
30	e	i
31	e	–

MOON TABLE 3

M/D	a	b	d	e	f	g	i
0	LI	LI	LI	SC	SC	SC	SA
1	LI	LI	SC	SC	SC	SA	SA
2	LI	SC	SC	SC	SA	SA	CP
3	SC	SC	SC	SA	SA	CP	CP
4	SC	SA	SA	SA	CP	CP	CP
5	SA	SA	SA	CP	CP	AQ	AQ
6	SA	CP	CP	CP	AQ	AQ	AQ
7	SA	CP	CP	AQ	AQ	PI	PI
8	CP	CP	CP	AQ	PI	PI	PI
9	CP	AQ	AQ	AQ	PI	PI	AR
10	AQ	AQ	AQ	PI	AR	AR	AR
11	AQ	PI	PI	PI	AR	AR	TA
12	PI	PI	PI	AR	TA	TA	TA
13	PI	AR	PI	AR	TA	TA	GE
14	AR	AR	AR	TA	GE	GE	GE
15	AR	AR	AR	TA	TA	TA	GE
16	AR	AR	TA	TA	GE	GE	GE
17	AR	TA	TA	GE	GE	GE	CA
18	TA	TA	GE	GE	GE	CA	CA
19	TA	TA	GE	GE	CA	CA	CA
20	GE	GE	GE	CA	CA	CA	LE
21	GE	GE	CA	CA	CA	LE	LE
22	GE	CA	CA	CA	LE	LE	VI
23	CA	CA	CA	LE	LE	LE	VI
24	CA	CA	LE	LE	LE	VI	VI
25	CA	LE	LE	LE	VI	VI	LI
26	LE	LE	VI	VI	VI	LI	LI
27	LE	VI	VI	VI	LI	LI	SC
28	VI	VI	VI	LI	LI	LI	SC
29	VI	VI	LI	LI	LI	SC	SC

AR = Aries, TA = Taurus, GE = Gemini, CA = Cancer, LE = Leo, VI = Virgo, LI = Libra, SC = Scorpio, SA = Sagittarius, CP = Capricorn, AQ = Aquarius, PI = Pisces

MOON SIGNS

Moon in Aries

You have a strong imagination, courage, determination and a desire to do things in your own way and forge your own path through life.

Originality is a key attribute; you are seldom stuck for ideas although your mind is changeable and you could take the time to focus on individual tasks. Often quick-tempered, you take orders from few people and live life at a fast pace. Avoid health problems by taking regular time out for rest and relaxation.

Emotionally, it is important that you talk to those you are closest to and work out your true feelings. Once you discover that people are there to help, there is less necessity for you to do everything yourself.

Moon in Taurus

The Moon in Taurus gives you a courteous and friendly manner, which means you are likely to have many friends.

The good things in life mean a lot to you, as Taurus is an Earth sign that delights in experiences which please the senses. Hence you are probably a lover of good food and drink, which may in turn mean you need to keep an eye on the bathroom scales, especially as looking good is also important to you.

Emotionally you are fairly stable and you stick by your own standards. Taureans do not respond well to change. Intuition also plays an important part in your life.

Moon in Gemini

You have a warm-hearted character, sympathetic and eager to help others. At times reserved, you can also be articulate and chatty: this is part of the paradox of Gemini, which always brings duplicity to the nature. You are interested in current affairs, have a good intellect, and are good company and likely to have many friends. Most of your friends have a high opinion of you and would be ready to defend you should the need arise. However, this is usually unnecessary, as you are quite capable of defending yourself in any verbal confrontation.

Travel is important to your inquisitive mind and you find intellectual stimulus in mixing with people from different cultures. You also gain much from reading, writing and the arts but you do need plenty of rest and relaxation in order to avoid fatigue.

Moon in Cancer

The Moon in Cancer at the time of birth is a fortunate position as Cancer is the Moon's natural home. This means that the qualities of compassion and understanding given by the Moon are especially enhanced in your nature, and you are friendly and sociable and cope well with emotional pressures. You cherish home and family life, and happily do the domestic tasks. Your surroundings are important to you and you hate squalor and filth. You are likely to have a love of music and poetry.

Your basic character, although at times changeable like the Moon itself, depends on symmetry. You aim to make your surroundings comfortable and harmonious, for yourself and those close to you.

Moon in Leo

The best qualities of the Moon and Leo come together to make you warm-hearted, fair, ambitious and self-confident. With good organisational abilities, you invariably rise to a position of responsibility in your chosen career. This is fortunate as you don't enjoy being an 'also-ran' and would rather be an important part of a small organisation than a menial in a large one.

You should be lucky in love, and happy, provided you put in the effort to make a comfortable home for yourself and those close to you. It is likely that you will have a love of pleasure, sport, music and literature. Life brings you many rewards, most of them as a direct result of your own efforts, although you may be luckier than average and ready to make the best of any situation.

Moon in Virgo

You are endowed with good mental abilities and a keen receptive memory, but you are never ostentatious or pretentious. Naturally quite reserved, you still have many friends, especially of the opposite sex. Marital relationships must be discussed carefully and worked at so that they remain harmonious, as personal attachments can be a problem if you do not give them your full attention.

Talented and persevering, you possess artistic qualities and are a good homemaker. Earning your honours through genuine merit, you work long and hard towards your objectives but show little pride in your achievements. Many short journeys will be undertaken in your life.

Moon in Libra

With the Moon in Libra you are naturally popular and make friends easily. People like you, probably more than you realise, you bring fun to a party and are a natural diplomat. For all its good points, Libra is not the most stable of astrological signs and, as a result, your emotions can be a little unstable too. Therefore, although the Moon in Libra is said to be good for love and marriage, your Sun sign and Rising sign will have an important effect on your emotional and loving qualities.

You must remember to relate to others in your decision-making. Co-operation is crucial because Libra represents the 'balance' of life that can only be achieved through harmonious relationships. Conformity is not easy for you because Libra, an Air sign, likes its independence.

Moon in Scorpio

Some people might call you pushy. In fact, all you really want to do is to live life to the full and protect yourself and your family from the pressures of life. Take care to avoid giving the impression of being sarcastic or impulsive and use your energies wisely and constructively.

You have great courage and you invariably achieve your goals by force of personality and sheer effort. You are fond of mystery and are good at predicting the outcome of situations and events. Travel experiences can be beneficial to you.

You may experience problems if you do not take time to examine your motives in a relationship, and also if you allow jealousy, always a feature of Scorpio, to cloud your judgement.

Moon in Sagittarius

The Moon in Sagittarius helps to make you a generous individual with humanitarian qualities and a kind heart. Restlessness may be intrinsic as your mind is seldom still. Perhaps because of this, you have a need for change that could lead you to several major moves during your adult life. You are not afraid to stand your ground when you know your judgement is right, you speak directly and have good intuition.

At work you are quick, efficient and versatile and so you make an ideal employee. You need work to be intellectually demanding and do not enjoy tedious routines.

In relationships, you anger quickly if faced with stupidity or deception, though you are just as quick to forgive and forget. Emotionally, there are times when your heart rules your head.

Moon in Capricorn

The Moon in Capricorn makes you popular and likely to come into the public eye in some way. The watery Moon is not entirely comfortable in the Earth sign of Capricorn and this may lead to some difficulties in the early years of life. An initial lack of creative ability and indecision must be overcome before the true qualities of patience and perseverance inherent in Capricorn can show through.

You have good administrative ability and are a capable worker, and if you are careful you can accumulate wealth. But you must be cautious and take professional advice in partnerships, as you are open to deception. You may be interested in social or welfare work, which suit your organisational skills and sympathy for others.

Moon in Aquarius

The Moon in Aquarius makes you an active and agreeable person with a friendly, easy-going nature. Sympathetic to the needs of others, you flourish in a laid-back atmosphere. You are broad-minded, fair and open to suggestion, although sometimes you have an unconventional quality which others can find hard to understand.

You are interested in the strange and curious, and in old articles and places. You enjoy trips to these places and gain much from them. Political, scientific and educational work interests you and you might choose a career in science or technology.

Money-wise, you make gains through innovation and concentration and Lunar Aquarians often tackle more than one job at a time. In love you are kind and honest.

Moon in Pisces

You have a kind, sympathetic nature, somewhat retiring at times, but you always take account of others' feelings and help when you can.

Personal relationships may be problematic, but as life goes on you can learn from your experiences and develop a better understanding of yourself and the world around you.

You have a fondness for travel, appreciate beauty and harmony and hate disorder and strife. You may be fond of literature and would make a good writer or speaker yourself. You have a creative imagination and may come across as an incurable romantic. You have strong intuition, maybe bordering on a mediumistic quality, which sets you apart from the mass. You may not be rich in cash terms, but your personal gifts are worth more than gold.

SCORPIO IN LOVE

Discover how compatible you are with people from the same and other parts of the zodiac. Five stars equals a match made in heaven!

Scorpio meets Scorpio

Scorpio is deep, complex and enigmatic, traits which often lead to misunderstanding with other zodiac signs, so a double Scorpio match can work well because both parties understand one another. They will allow each other periods of silence and reflection but still be willing to help, advise and support when necessary. Their relationship may seem odd to others but that doesn't matter if those involved are happy. All in all, an unusual but contented combination. Star rating: *****

Scorpio meets Sagittarius

Sagittarius needs constant stimulation and loves to be busy from dawn till dusk which may mean that it feels rather frustrated by Scorpio. Scorpions are hard workers, too, but they are also contemplative and need periods of quiet which may mean that they appear dull to Sagittarius. This could lead to a gulf between the two which must be overcome. With time and patience on both sides, this can be a lucrative encounter and good in terms of home and family. A variable alliance. Star rating: ***

Scorpio meets Capricorn

Lack of communication is the governing factor here. Neither of this pair are renowned communicators and both need a partner to draw out their full verbal potential. Consequently, Scorpio may find Capricorn cold and unapproachable while Capricorn could find Scorpio dark and brooding. Both are naturally tidy and would keep a pristine house but great effort and a mutual goal is needed on both sides to overcome the missing spark. A good match on the financial side, but probably not an earthshattering personal encounter. Star rating: **

Scorpio meets Aquarius

This is a promising and practical combination. Scorpio responds well to Aquarius' exploration of its deep nature and so this shy sign becomes lighter, brighter and more inspirational. Meanwhile, Aquarians are rarely as sure of themselves as they like to appear and are reassured by Scorpio's steady and determined support. Both signs want to be kind to the other which is a basis for a relationship that should be warm most of the time and extremely hot occasionally. Star rating: ****

Scorpio meets Pisces

If ever there were two zodiac signs that have a total rapport, it has to be Scorpio and Pisces. They share very similar needs: they are not gregarious and are happy with a little silence, good music and time to contemplate the finer things in life, and both are attracted to family life. Apart, they can have a tendency to wander in a romantic sense, but this is reduced when they come together. They are deep, firm friends who enjoy each other's company and this must lead to an excellent chance of success. These people are surely made for each other! Star rating: *****

Scorpio meets Aries

There can be great affection here, even if the two signs are so very different. The common link is the planet Mars, which plays a part in both these natures. Although Aries is, outwardly, the most dominant, Scorpio people are among the most powerful to be found anywhere. This quiet determination is respected by Aries. Aries will satisfy the passionate side of Scorpio, particularly with instruction from Scorpio. There are mysteries here which will add spice to life. The few arguments that do occur are likely to be awe-inspiring. Star rating: ****

Scorpio meets Taurus

Scorpio is deep – very deep – which may be a problem, because Taurus doesn't wear its heart on its sleeve either. It might be difficult for this pair to get together, because neither is naturally inclined to make the first move. Taurus stands in awe of the power and intensity of the Scorpio mind, while the Scorpion is interested in the Bull's affable and friendly qualities, so an enduring relationship could be forged if the couple ever get round to talking. Both are lovers of home and family, which will help to cement a relationship. Star rating: **

Scorpio meets Gemini

There could be problems here. Scorpio is one of the deepest and least understood of all the zodiac signs, which at first seems like a challenge to intellectual Gemini, who thinks it can solve anything. But the deeper the Gemini digs, the further down Scorpio goes. Meanwhile, Scorpio may be finding Gemini thoughtless, shallow and even downright annoying. Gemini is often afraid of Scorpio's perception and strength, together with the sting in the Scorpion's tail. Anything is possible, but the outlook for this match is less than promising. Star rating: **

Scorpio meets Cancer

This match is potentially a great success, a fact which is often a mystery to astrologers. Some feel it is due to the compatibility of the Water element, but it could also come from a mixture of similarity and difference in the personalities. Scorpio is partly ruled by Mars, which gives it a deep, passionate, dominant and powerful side. Cancerians generally like and respect this amalgam, and recognise something there that they would like to adopt themselves. On the other side of the coin, Scorpio needs love and emotional security which Cancer offers generously. Star rating: *****

Scorpio meets Leo

Stand back and watch the sparks fly! Scorpio has the deep sensitivity of a Water sign but it is also partially ruled by Fire planet Mars, from which it draws great power, and Leo will find that difficult. Leo loves to take charge and really hates to feel psychologically undermined, which is Scorpio's stock-in-trade. Scorpio may find Leo's ideals a little shallow, which will be upsetting to the Lion. Anything is possible, but this possibility is rather slimmer than most. Star rating: **

Scorpio meets Virgo

There are one or two potential difficulties here, but there is also a meeting point from which to overcome them. Virgo is very caring and protective, a trait which Scorpio understands and even emulates. Scorpio will impress Virgo with its serious side. Both signs are consistent, although also sarcastic. Scorpio may uncover a hidden passion in Virgo which all too often lies deep within its Earth-sign nature. Material success is very likely, with Virgo taking the lion's share of the domestic chores and family responsibilities. Star rating: ***

Scorpio meets Libra

Many astrologers have reservations about this match because, on the surface, the signs are so different. However, this couple may find fulfilment because these differences mean that their respective needs are met. Scorpio needs a partner to lighten the load, which won't daunt Libra, while Libra looks for a steadfast quality which it doesn't possess, but which Scorpio can supply naturally. Financial success is possible because they both have good ideas and back them up with hard work and determination. All in all, a promising outlook. Star rating: ****

VENUS:
THE PLANET OF LOVE

If you look up at the sky around sunset or sunrise you will often see Venus in close attendance to the Sun. It is arguably one of the most beautiful sights of all and there is little wonder that historically it became associated with the goddess of love. But although Venus does play an important part in the way you view love and in the way others see you romantically, this is only one of the spheres of influence that it enjoys in your overall character.

Venus has a part to play in the more cultured side of your life and has much to do with your appreciation of art, literature, music and general creativity. Even the way you look is responsive to the part of the zodiac that Venus occupied at the start of your life, though this fact is also down to your Sun sign and Ascending sign. If, at the time you were born, Venus occupied one of the more gregarious zodiac signs, you will be more likely to wear your heart on your sleeve, as well as to be more attracted to entertainment, social gatherings and good company. If on the other hand Venus occupied a quiet zodiac sign at the time of your birth, you would tend to be more retiring and less willing to shine in public situations.

It's good to know what part the planet Venus plays in your life for it can have a great bearing on the way you appear to the rest of the world and since we all have to mix with others, you can learn to make the very best of what Venus has to offer you.

One of the great complications in the past has always been trying to establish exactly what zodiac position Venus enjoyed when you were born because the planet is notoriously difficult to track. However, we have solved that problem by creating a table that is exclusive to your Sun sign, which you will find on the following page.

Establishing your Venus sign could not be easier. Just look up the year of your birth on the next page and you will see a sign of the zodiac. This was the sign that Venus occupied in the period covered by your sign in that year. If Venus occupied more than one sign during the period, this is indicated by the date on which the sign changed, and the name of the new sign. For instance, if you were born in 1950, Venus was in Libra until the 28th October, after which time it was in Scorpio. If you were born before 28th October your Venus sign is Libra, if you were born on or after 28th October, your Venus sign is Scorpio. Once you have established the position of Venus at the time of your birth, you can then look in the pages which follow to see how this has a bearing on your life as a whole.

1909 SAGITTARIUS / 7.11 CAPRICORN
1910 LIBRA / 30.10 SCORPIO
1911 VIRGO / 9.11 LIBRA
1912 SCORPIO / 24.10 SAGITTARIUS /
    18.11 CAPRICORN
1913 LIBRA / 14.11 SCORPIO
1914 SAGITTARIUS / 16.11 SCORPIO
1915 SCORPIO / 9.11 SAGITTARIUS
1916 VIRGO / 3.11 LIBRA
1917 SAGITTARIUS / 7.11 CAPRICORN
1918 LIBRA / 30.10 SCORPIO
1919 VIRGO / 9.11 LIBRA
1920 SCORPIO / 24.10 SAGITTARIUS /
    17.11 CAPRICORN
1921 LIBRA / 14.11 SCORPIO
1922 SAGITTARIUS / 16.11 SCORPIO
1923 SCORPIO / 9.11 SAGITTARIUS
1924 VIRGO / 3.11 LIBRA
1925 SAGITTARIUS / 7.11 CAPRICORN
1926 LIBRA / 29.10 SCORPIO
1927 VIRGO / 10.11 LIBRA
1928 SAGITTARIUS /
    17.11 CAPRICORN
1929 LIBRA / 13.11 SCORPIO
1930 SAGITTARIUS / 16.11 SCORPIO
1931 SCORPIO / 8.11 SAGITTARIUS
1932 VIRGO / 2.11 LIBRA
1933 SAGITTARIUS / 7.11 CAPRICORN
1934 LIBRA / 29.10 SCORPIO
1935 VIRGO / 10.11 LIBRA
1936 SAGITTARIUS / 16.11 CAPRICORN
1937 LIBRA / 13.11 SCORPIO
1938 SAGITTARIUS / 16.11 SCORPIO
1939 SCORPIO / 7.11 SAGITTARIUS
1940 VIRGO / 2.11 LIBRA
1941 SAGITTARIUS / 7.11 CAPRICORN
1942 LIBRA / 28.10 SCORPIO
1943 VIRGO / 10.11 LIBRA
1944 SAGITTARIUS / 16.11 CAPRICORN
1945 LIBRA / 13.11 SCORPIO
1946 SAGITTARIUS / 16.11 SCORPIO
1947 SCORPIO / 6.11 SAGITTARIUS
1948 VIRGO / 1.11 LIBRA
1949 SAGITTARIUS / 6.11 CAPRICORN
1950 LIBRA / 28.10 SCORPIO
1951 VIRGO / 10.11 LIBRA
1952 SAGITTARIUS / 16.11 CAPRICORN
1953 LIBRA / 12.11 SCORPIO
1954 SAGITTARIUS / 28.10 SCORPIO
1955 SCORPIO / 6.11 SAGITTARIUS
1956 VIRGO / 1.11 LIBRA
1957 SAGITTARIUS / 6.11 CAPRICORN
1958 LIBRA / 27.10 SCORPIO
1959 VIRGO / 10.11 LIBRA

1960 SAGITTARIUS /
    15.11 CAPRICORN
1961 LIBRA / 12.11 SCORPIO
1962 SAGITTARIUS / 28.10 SCORPIO
1963 SCORPIO / 5.11 SAGITTARIUS
1964 VIRGO / 31.10 LIBRA
1965 SAGITTARIUS / 6.11 CAPRICORN
1966 LIBRA / 27.10 SCORPIO
1967 VIRGO / 10.11 LIBRA
1968 SAGITTARIUS /
    15.11 CAPRICORN
1969 LIBRA / 11.11 SCORPIO
1970 SAGITTARIUS / 28.10 SCORPIO
1971 SCORPIO / 4.11 SAGITTARIUS
1972 VIRGO / 31.10 LIBRA
1973 SAGITTARIUS / 6.11 CAPRICORN
1974 LIBRA / 26.10 SCORPIO
1975 VIRGO / 9.11 LIBRA
1976 SAGITTARIUS /
    15.11 CAPRICORN
1977 LIBRA / 11.11 SCORPIO
1978 SAGITTARIUS / 28.10 SCORPIO
1979 SCORPIO / 4.11 SAGITTARIUS
1980 VIRGO / 30.10 LIBRA
1981 SAGITTARIUS / 5.11 CAPRICORN
1982 LIBRA / 26.10 SCORPIO
1983 VIRGO / 9.11 LIBRA
1984 SAGITTARIUS /
    14.11 CAPRICORN
1985 LIBRA / 10.11 SCORPIO
1986 SAGITTARIUS / 28.10 SCORPIO
1987 SCORPIO / 3.11 SAGITTARIUS
1988 VIRGO / 30.10 LIBRA
1989 SAGITTARIUS / 5.11 CAPRICORN
1990 LIBRA / 25.10 SCORPIO
1991 VIRGO / 9.11 LIBRA
1992 SAGITTARIUS /
    14.11 CAPRICORN
1993 LIBRA / 10.11 SCORPIO
1994 SAGITTARIUS / 28.10 SCORPIO
1995 SCORPIO / 3.11 SAGITTARIUS
1996 VIRGO / 29.10 LIBRA
1997 SAGITTARIUS / 5.11 CAPRICORN
1998 LIBRA / 25.10 SCORPIO
1999 VIRGO / 9.11 LIBRA
2000 SAGITTARIUS /
    14.11 CAPRICORN
2001 LIBRA / 10.11 SCORPIO
2002 SAGITTARIUS / 28.10 SCORPIO
2003 SCORPIO / 3.11 SAGITTARIUS
2004 VIRGO / 29.10 LIBRA
2005 SAGITTARIUS / 5.11 CAPRICORN
2006 LIBRA / 25.10 SCORPIO
2007 VIRGO / 9.11 LIBRA

VENUS THROUGH THE ZODIAC SIGNS

Venus in Aries

Amongst other things, the position of Venus in Aries indicates a fondness for travel, music and all creative pursuits. Your nature tends to be affectionate and you would try not to create confusion or difficulty for others if it could be avoided. Many people with this planetary position have a great love of the theatre, and mental stimulation is of the greatest importance. Early romantic attachments are common with Venus in Aries, so it is very important to establish a genuine sense of romantic continuity. Early marriage is not recommended, especially if it is based on sympathy. You may give your heart a little too readily on occasions.

Venus in Taurus

You are capable of very deep feelings and your emotions tend to last for a very long time. This makes you a trusting partner and lover, whose constancy is second to none. In life you are precise and careful and always try to do things the right way. Although this means an ordered life, which you are comfortable with, it can also lead you to be rather too fussy for your own good. Despite your pleasant nature, you are very fixed in your opinions and quite able to speak your mind. Others are attracted to you and historical astrologers always quoted this position of Venus as being very fortunate in terms of marriage. However, if you find yourself involved in a failed relationship, it could take you a long time to trust again.

Venus in Gemini

As with all associations related to Gemini, you tend to be quite versatile, anxious for change and intelligent in your dealings with the world at large. You may gain money from more than one source but you are equally good at spending it. There is an inference here that you are a good communicator, via either the written or the spoken word, and you love to be in the company of interesting people. Always on the look-out for culture, you may also be very fond of music, and love to indulge the curious and cultured side of your nature. In romance you tend to have more than one relationship and could find yourself associated with someone who has previously been a friend or even a distant relative.

Venus in Cancer

You often stay close to home because you are very fond of family and enjoy many of your most treasured moments when you are with those you love. Being naturally sympathetic, you will always do anything you can to support those around you, even people you hardly know at all. This charitable side of your nature is your most noticeable trait and is one of the reasons why others are naturally so fond of you. Being receptive and in some cases even psychic, you can see through to the soul of most of those with whom you come into contact. You may not commence too many romantic attachments but when you do give your heart, it tends to be unconditionally.

Venus in Leo

It must become quickly obvious to almost anyone you meet that you are kind, sympathetic and yet determined enough to stand up for anyone or anything that is truly important to you. Bright and sunny, you warm the world with your natural enthusiasm and would rarely do anything to hurt those around you, or at least not intentionally. In romance you are ardent and sincere, though some may find your style just a little overpowering. Gains come through your contacts with other people and this could be especially true with regard to romance, for love and money often come hand in hand for those who were born with Venus in Leo. People claim to understand you, though you are more complex than you seem.

Venus in Virgo

Your nature could well be fairly quiet no matter what your Sun sign might be, though this fact often manifests itself as an inner peace and would not prevent you from being basically sociable. Some delays and even the odd disappointment in love cannot be ruled out with this planetary position, though it's a fact that you will usually find the happiness you look for in the end. Catapulting yourself into romantic entanglements that you know to be rather ill-advised is not sensible, and it would be better to wait before you committed yourself exclusively to any one person. It is the essence of your nature to serve the world at large and through doing so it is possible that you will attract money at some stage in your life.

Venus in Libra

Venus is very comfortable in Libra and bestows upon those people who have this planetary position a particular sort of kindness that is easy to recognise. This is a very good position for all sorts of friendships and also for romantic attachments that usually bring much joy into your life. Few individuals with Venus in Libra would avoid marriage and since you are capable of great depths of love, it is likely that you will find a contented personal life. You like to mix with people of integrity and intelligence but don't take kindly to scruffy surroundings or work that means getting your hands too dirty. Careful speculation, good business dealings and money through marriage all seem fairly likely.

Venus in Scorpio

You are quite open and tend to spend money quite freely, even on those occasions when you don't have very much. Although your intentions are always good, there are times when you get yourself in to the odd scrape and this can be particularly true when it comes to romance, which you may come to late or from a rather unexpected direction. Certainly you have the power to be happy and to make others contented on the way, but you find the odd stumbling block on your journey through life and it could seem that you have to work harder than those around you. As a result of this, you gain a much deeper understanding of the true value of personal happiness than many people ever do, and are likely to achieve true contentment in the end.

Venus in Sagittarius

You are lighthearted, cheerful and always able to see the funny side of any situation. These facts enhance your popularity, which is especially high with members of the opposite sex. You should never have to look too far to find romantic interest in your life, though it is just possible that you might be too willing to commit yourself before you are certain that the person in question is right for you. Part of the problem here extends to other areas of life too. The fact is that you like variety in everything and so can tire of situations that fail to offer it. All the same, if you choose wisely and learn to understand your restless side, then great happiness can be yours.

Venus in Capricorn

The most notable trait that comes from Venus in this position is that it makes you trustworthy and able to take on all sorts of responsibilities in life. People are instinctively fond of you and love you all the more because you are always ready to help those who are in any form of need. Social and business popularity can be yours and there is a magnetic quality to your nature that is particularly attractive in a romantic sense. Anyone who wants a partner for a lover, a spouse and a good friend too would almost certainly look in your direction. Constancy is the hallmark of your nature and unfaithfulness would go right against the grain. You might sometimes be a little too trusting.

Venus in Aquarius

This location of Venus offers a fondness for travel and a desire to try out something new at every possible opportunity. You are extremely easy to get along with and tend to have many friends from varied backgrounds, classes and inclinations. You like to live a distinct sort of life and gain a great deal from moving about, both in a career sense and with regard to your home. It is not out of the question that you could form a romantic attachment to someone who comes from far away or be attracted to a person of a distinctly artistic and original nature. What you cannot stand is jealousy, for you have friends of both sexes and would want to keep things that way.

Venus in Pisces

The first thing people tend to notice about you is your wonderful, warm smile. Being very charitable by nature you will do anything to help others, even if you don't know them well. Much of your life may be spent sorting out situations for other people, but it is very important to feel that you are living for yourself too. In the main, you remain cheerful, and tend to be quite attractive to members of the opposite sex. Where romantic attachments are concerned, you could be drawn to people who are significantly older or younger than yourself or to someone with a unique career or point of view. It might be best for you to avoid marrying whilst you are still very young.

SCORPIO:
2006 DIARY PAGES

October

2006

1 SUNDAY
Moon Age Day 9   Moon Sign Capricorn

There is much about today that could seem quite comfortable, but at the same time little niggles, mainly to do with family issues could arise. Originality is the key to ultimate success and you might also be anxious to get things done in and around your home. A day to avoid unnecessary complications with friends.

2 MONDAY
Moon Age Day 10   Moon Sign Aquarius

Not only is the Sun in your solar twelfth house, but the planet Venus is there too. This is unlikely to bring many reassurances to personal relationships, some of which you are looking at rather negatively. It's important to remember what is real and those things that exist mainly inside your own head.

3 TUESDAY
Moon Age Day 11   Moon Sign Aquarius

Beware of possible deception today, which could come from any direction. It might be that you are being misled by people who are themselves in the dark, and some investigation is clearly called for. Periods of enjoyment could come from the strangest directions right now, but don't knock it!

4 WEDNESDAY
Moon Age Day 12   Moon Sign Pisces

This is one of the best times during October to engage in social activities. 'The more, the merrier' can be your present adage and you might even decide to smile upon those you haven't cared for very much in the past. You can be quite flexible in your attitude at present, which certain of your friends will probably find a relief.

5 THURSDAY
Moon Age Day 13   Moon Sign Pisces

Your general position could seem weaker right now, particularly if you are not looking at things as positively as you might. It is important to believe in yourself and not to allow little failures to fill your mind. If things do go wrong, your best response at present is to pick up the pieces and start again immediately.

6 FRIDAY
Moon Age Day 14   Moon Sign Pisces

If the brakes seem to be applied where progress at work is concerned, you might decide to turn your mind in the direction of romantic and social trends, both of which should be better. A day to leave practical jobs alone as much as you can and concentrate almost entirely on enjoying yourself in good company.

7 SATURDAY
Moon Age Day 15   Moon Sign Aries

Love issues might seem more trouble than they are worth on occasion today, but you know in your own heart that this is not the case. If you feel as though you are taking something of a battering at the moment, why not turn to a good friend and laugh away your little troubles in their company? You will probably feel great as a result.

8 SUNDAY
Moon Age Day 16   Moon Sign Aries

Emotions can still be a little raw, but today is better for money and for any practical decisions that have to be made. If you can get some change into your day, then so much the better. Anything cultural would really grab your imagination and can offer the sort of diversion that is exactly what you need.

9 MONDAY
Moon Age Day 17   Moon Sign Taurus

You might find a few difficulties coming your way today, probably as a result of the way those around you are reacting. Accept that this is part of the present astrological line-up and don't take too much notice of the situation. There are still some gains to be made, particularly in romantic attachments and through simple friendship.

10 TUESDAY   *Moon Age Day 18   Moon Sign Taurus*

Another potentially quiet day, at least at the beginning of it. Later on the Moon moves out of your zodiac sign and you should feel more like taking on the world. Try not to be too pushy regarding an idea you have at work, but bring others round to your point of view in a very steady and deliberate way.

11 WEDNESDAY   *Moon Age Day 19   Moon Sign Gemini*

This is a period during which you have scope to take the emotional side of life fairly seriously. You might be just a little too sensitive for your own good on occasions and you need to be aware of the high regard that others have for you. Not a good day for any real financial risk.

12 THURSDAY   *Moon Age Day 20   Moon Sign Gemini*

There could be some pressure being placed upon you to review recent happenings and to react in a slightly more flexible way. Scorpio can be quite fixed in its attitudes sometimes and it wouldn't do any harm to give a little. Any arrangements for a journey in the medium-term future are now positively highlighted.

13 FRIDAY   *Moon Age Day 21   Moon Sign Cancer*

The general pace of life may seem to be slowing a little, but that doesn't really apply to the more social aspects that are on offer later in the day. You can afford to take full advantage of any chance to get out on the town, possibly with friends, and should avoid spending all your spare time in front of the television.

14 SATURDAY   *Moon Age Day 22   Moon Sign Cancer*

Being outdoors would probably stimulate you more than anything else today and the further you are from civilisation, the better you are likely to feel. A trip to the coast might suit you fine, especially if you are in the company of someone you find both interesting and attractive.

15 SUNDAY *Moon Age Day 23   Moon Sign Leo*

Look out for a phase in your love life during which communication could be something of a problem. As long as you realise this fact and take the appropriate steps, you can make sure that all is well. What you don't want to be accused of is playing all your cards too close to your chest.

16 MONDAY *Moon Age Day 24   Moon Sign Leo*

It might be entirely appropriate to get a little peace and quiet today. The Sun is still in your solar twelfth house and it stays there until after the 20th of the month. This alone is inclined to make you more pensive but it doesn't mean you fail to make any sort of progress. Movement can come as much through thinking as doing now.

17 TUESDAY *Moon Age Day 25   Moon Sign Virgo*

You have scope to be a good deal more carefree and easygoing, thanks to the present position of the Moon. These rapidly changing trends might make you appear to be somewhat Mercurial when viewed by others, but it doesn't do any harm at all to keep people guessing now and again.

18 WEDNESDAY *Moon Age Day 26   Moon Sign Virgo*

You need to be where the action is, especially when it comes to the more practical side of life. If you don't get yourself involved, others might be making decisions on your behalf, and that is not something you would want. In everyday life you could be breaking rules, or at the very least bending them significantly.

19 THURSDAY *Moon Age Day 27   Moon Sign Virgo*

Trends indicate that a situation created within your love life might prove to be troublesome and more than a little frustrating. This may come about if your partner or sweetheart hears what you are saying but misconstrues your meaning. Your best response is to explain your point of view in a fuller and less ambiguous way.

20 FRIDAY
Moon Age Day 28   Moon Sign Libra

It seems as though you may be rather easy to influence at the moment, which means you could be taken advantage of. You would be wise to keep your purse or wallet closed for the moment and understand that with both the Sun and the Moon now in your solar twelfth house, you might be rather too insular and unapproachable for your own good.

21 SATURDAY
Moon Age Day 0   Moon Sign Libra

Another slightly quieter day is possible but there is a gradual build-up of much better astrological trends on the way, and you can take advantage of this as Saturday progresses. A day to opt for something different if you can and avoid getting tied down with family matters that though important could prove tedious.

22 SUNDAY
Moon Age Day 1   Moon Sign Scorpio

There is fun to be had today, not to mention the possibility of displaying the most dynamic quality of your nature that has shown all month. The lunar high helps you to get what you want and points you in the direction of a very positive start to the new working week tomorrow.

23 MONDAY
Moon Age Day 2   Moon Sign Scorpio

Take advantage of the fact that Lady Luck is on your side. It should be easy to make up your mind about anything today, and if you are positive in your approach, you can get practically everyone to believe your point of view to be correct. There is more than a little creative genius about you right now.

24 TUESDAY
Moon Age Day 3   Moon Sign Scorpio

For the third day in a row fortune has potential to smile on you. In addition, the Sun is now also in a much better position to give you what you want. The most noticeable difference between now and the earlier days of the month is that you can radiate confidence, both for yourself and on account of others.

25 WEDNESDAY   *Moon Age Day 4   Moon Sign Sagittarius*

Beware of acting on pure impulse. There is a great deal happening in your solar first house just at present and this includes the position there of the planet Mars. This could incline you to be a little too rash for your own good and might even lead to unnecessary and slightly dangerous risks. Stop and think first.

26 THURSDAY   *Moon Age Day 5   Moon Sign Sagittarius*

You can make a very big impact on someone at the moment and should be quite certain about your attitude to almost anything. Positive thinking allows you to get in a position to overturn difficulties that were evident a few days ago, and you have it within you to sell fridges to Eskimos if you've a mind to do so.

27 FRIDAY   *Moon Age Day 6   Moon Sign Capricorn*

Amongst a plethora of planets, Venus is also in your solar first house at the present time. This can have a pleasant effect on relationships, both personal and more social ones. You can persuade people to like you and to let the fact be known. There are possible financial gains to be made as a result of canny actions on your behalf.

28 SATURDAY   ☿ *Moon Age Day 7   Moon Sign Capricorn*

Communications are boosted even more and this is a time during which you can see good in just about anything. You will need to be just a little circumspect before taking on more than you can reasonably manage. It probably isn't now that the chickens come home to roost, but a week or more into the future.

29 SUNDAY   ☿ *Moon Age Day 8   Moon Sign Aquarius*

Taking yourself too much for granted is not to be recommended at the moment. It seems that your best laid plans can go slightly wrong and that would put a definite dent in your present confidence. Even Scorpio can't always do the impossible, at least not without gathering a little help from your friends.

30 MONDAY   ☿ *Moon Age Day 9   Moon Sign Aquarius*

You should have what it takes to get where you want to be in a general sense and shouldn't have too many problems persuading the world that you know what you are talking about. Silver-tongued and enchanting, you have scope to make yourself more popular at this stage of the month than has been the case for weeks.

31 TUESDAY   ☿ *Moon Age Day 10   Moon Sign Aquarius*

A good boost could come along thanks to your friends and the way they look at your needs. Be willing to accept that someone might know better than you do regarding a specific issue, and don't be shy of taking on the specific skills of anyone who is now in a position to help you.

November

2006

1 WEDNESDAY   ☿   *Moon Age Day 11   Moon Sign Pisces*

You should certainly know how to enjoy yourself at the moment and the first day of a new month offers a chance for you to move closer than ever to achieving a specific objective that is very important to you. Romance looks good too, and particularly so for any Scorpios who have recently started a new relationship.

2 THURSDAY   ☿   *Moon Age Day 12   Moon Sign Pisces*

Daily matters might not only keep you happily on the go but could also contain much interesting information. Virtually nothing should pass you by right now and you can make a silk purse out of a sow's ear in quite a number of ways. You might have a secret admirer, which although gratifying in one way could be embarrassing in another.

3 FRIDAY   ☿   *Moon Age Day 13   Moon Sign Aries*

You are still in the middle of a high-energy period and can afford to take on a number of different tasks. Action and adventure are well accented, and although it is getting somewhat late in the year you would do well in any outdoors activity. Sporting Scorpios are the luckiest of all now!

4 SATURDAY   ☿   *Moon Age Day 14   Moon Sign Aries*

Even if ambitions remain strong at the moment, you really need to be looking at life's finer details. Attitude is very important when approaching others and especially so if you want to get them on your side. You can progress quite well, but the fact that this is the weekend might get in the way somewhat.

5 SUNDAY ☿ *Moon Age Day 15   Moon Sign Taurus*

Things are inclined to slow a little as the lunar low encourages you into a more introspective phase. This might not be so easy to take at a time when you are generally quite progressive in your thinking You can best avoid impatience by realising that any setbacks are temporary in nature and shouldn't do anything to restrict you in the longer term.

6 MONDAY ☿ *Moon Age Day 16   Moon Sign Taurus*

You may decide to put objectives on the back burner for the moment and simply to relax a little. By tomorrow the lunar low will be out of the way, but in the meantime why not let others take some of the strain? You can still work hard but it might be difficult to make much in the way of progress.

7 TUESDAY ☿ *Moon Age Day 17   Moon Sign Gemini*

A rather self-assertive and quite a restless period is now at hand and this comes courtesy of the present position of the planet Mars. You would be wise not to lose your temper over issues that really are not worth the bother, and to use a little patience, especially when you are dealing with younger people.

8 WEDNESDAY ☿ *Moon Age Day 18   Moon Sign Gemini*

This is a time when it could be best simply to buckle down and get on with some work. You can achieve a great deal, but not without putting in the necessary effort. Trends indicate that comfort and security mean little or nothing to you for the remainder of this week. You can easily tackle several different jobs at the same time.

9 THURSDAY ☿ *Moon Age Day 19   Moon Sign Cancer*

You should be able to show a very pleasant disposition to the world at large, and even if you are busy you can find the time to make those around you happy. They in turn should take significant notice of you and listen very carefully to those Scorpio ideas. You instinctively know what looks and feels right around now.

10 FRIDAY   ☿   *Moon Age Day 20*   *Moon Sign Cancer*

The Sun is now very strong in your solar first house, bringing a time when you can ensure you are noticed by others. Don't be surprised if you attract compliments from fairly unexpected directions, and be willing to give of your best if you are put on show in some way.

11 SATURDAY   ☿   *Moon Age Day 21*   *Moon Sign Leo*

You need to concentrate today if you really want to get on, but if you are not at work the picture will look significantly different. Social trends are also good and you can continue to turn heads when it matters. An outing of some sort this evening might suit you down to the ground, especially if you can take good friends along.

12 SUNDAY   ☿   *Moon Age Day 22*   *Moon Sign Leo*

Your present impulsive manner could lead to a few unnecessary accidents and all of these can probably be avoided if you just look before you leap. The time is right to give of your best in social settings and to prove to others that you are something very special. Personalities tend to crop up all the time around now.

13 MONDAY   ☿   *Moon Age Day 23*   *Moon Sign Virgo*

You often enjoy attending to the needs of others, but perhaps never more so than seems to be the case right now. However, you need to take as well as give, so don't get too embarrassed if someone wants to make a big fuss of you. It's important to avoid any jealousy where your partner or someone you really fancy is concerned.

14 TUESDAY   ☿   *Moon Age Day 24*   *Moon Sign Virgo*

You are much more effective today than might seem to be the case, which is why you sometimes have to stand back and look at the way things are going. Although you can be efficient and swift, there is really no race, and it is quite important to enjoy the journey as well as the destination around this time.

15 WEDNESDAY ☿ *Moon Age Day 25 Moon Sign Virgo*

If you are involved with group activities today you should be in your element. At the moment you have the potential to be a very good team player, though you shouldn't be in the least surprised if the rest of the team look to you for advice. Routines are for the birds and you might even make things up as you go along.

16 THURSDAY ☿ *Moon Age Day 26 Moon Sign Libra*

A domestic matter may prove tiresome in certain ways, one of which is specific feelings that rise to the surface. Perhaps you need to clear the air and put someone in the picture about something they really don't understand. Activity is the key to success, so don't sit around in the shadows at all today.

17 FRIDAY ☿ *Moon Age Day 27 Moon Sign Libra*

Avoid confrontations that are brought about as a result of your ego, which is extremely well emphasised at the moment. You have what it takes to continue your present successful phase, but not if you insist on falling out over details. A day to let others have their say and then make up your mind.

18 SATURDAY ☿ *Moon Age Day 28 Moon Sign Scorpio*

Taking the initiative is most important now, at a time when most aspects of life are positively highlighted. The lunar high gives you extra scope for advancements and adds that degree of luck that is very important. The weekend has great potential to go with a swing and mostly because of the effort you put in.

19 SUNDAY *Moon Age Day 29 Moon Sign Scorpio*

Make the world your own by showing the very best qualities of which Scorpio is capable. You can be loyal, brave, adventurous and deeply magnetic. If you can't get others to do your bidding right now you probably are not trying hard enough. You would be wise to utilise your intuition when assessing the nature of newcomers.

20 MONDAY *Moon Age Day 0   Moon Sign Scorpio*

Once again you start the day with the Moon in your own zodiac sign. You need to be quite determined because some of the greatest potentials of the year lie around you now. Don't get bogged down with details that really are not that important, and insist that those in the know are listening to what you say.

21 TUESDAY *Moon Age Day 1   Moon Sign Sagittarius*

The potential for making money is still around, but unfortunately so is the possibility of losing it! It's all a matter of balance and you can't afford to gamble as much as you have been doing. Although you are in a position to stand up for yourself at this time, it is possible that you will be going a little too far.

22 WEDNESDAY *Moon Age Day 2   Moon Sign Sagittarius*

Financial matters may seem slightly rosier today, particularly if you are being more careful, but also if you are using the luck that is available. Romance is likely to be on your mind and you could discover that you have a secret admirer. Whether or not this realisation pleases you remains to be seen.

23 THURSDAY *Moon Age Day 3   Moon Sign Capricorn*

Once again you could prove to be decidedly lucky where money is concerned. The Sun has now moved into your solar second house, which is good for all cash-related matters. With plenty to crow about, you can afford to sing your own praises in the certain knowledge that those around you will allow you the luxury.

24 FRIDAY *Moon Age Day 4   Moon Sign Capricorn*

Trends suggest that your thinking is sharp and that your hunches are likely to be spot on in most situations. The only area of life in which you would be wise to exhibit a little care is domestically. It could be that your nearest and dearest don't have quite the regard for your opinions that they once had, or at least it might seem that way.

25 SATURDAY *Moon Age Day 5   Moon Sign Aquarius*

Powerful energies are at large and could rise to the surface at any time. You have what it takes to overcome any obstacles arising at work and to stun others with the strength of your hunches. You tend to be very reasonable, which is one of the reasons why your popularity is still very much in evidence.

26 SUNDAY *Moon Age Day 6   Moon Sign Aquarius*

Today could be rather less than satisfying at home, and especially so if you fail to take into account the opinions of those with whom you live. All in all, it might be better to spend some time away from home. Maybe a pre-Christmas shopping spree would take your fancy or a journey to a place of great interest.

27 MONDAY *Moon Age Day 7   Moon Sign Aquarius*

Financial trends assist you to progress, though you might have to be fairly circumspect when it comes to standing up for yourself because you can give offence very easily. Scorpio can be quite brusque and cutting at times, and this appears to be one of them. You might have to settle for second-best on at least one occasion.

28 TUESDAY *Moon Age Day 8   Moon Sign Pisces*

You can benefit from being demonstrative in a love relationship and by continuing to show a strongly extroverted attitude generally. Money matters are well accented, though you might decide to put something by with Christmas now being so close. There are definite gains to be made in terms of simple friendship.

29 WEDNESDAY *Moon Age Day 9   Moon Sign Pisces*

High spirits are very much in evidence around now and your general enthusiasm prevails. You have scope to demonstrate just how good you are when mixing with lots of different sorts of people and how much attention you can attract. Look out for a chance of meeting someone soon who has been something of an idol.

30 THURSDAY
Moon Age Day 10   Moon Sign Aries

You should see financial issues on a continuing upswing. This is not only a time to build successfully on previous efforts but also a period during which you can afford to back your most recent hunches. Gains can be made in some fairly unexpected places, like junk shops or market stalls for example.

December

2006

1 FRIDAY
Moon Age Day 11   Moon Sign Aries

A day to concentrate on firming up securities and capitalising on any recent successes. This would be a good time for financial planning and for making investments. The really progressive phase of the last few days is about to come to an abrupt end, so make the most of what is on offer today.

2 SATURDAY
Moon Age Day 12   Moon Sign Taurus

Even if things are still OK generally, you could well notice a great slowing of pace today. The lunar low is the culprit, and your best response is probably to relax and wait for a couple of days. If you take this weekend at face value and find pleasure where it naturally arises, you may not even notice the slower pace.

3 SUNDAY
Moon Age Day 13   Moon Sign Taurus

Don't expect to get too much out of life for the moment, but be willing to accept what comes your way. There's a slightly lazy streak to Scorpio, which is quite necessary on occasions. Leisure and pleasure remain important, but what probably pleases you most at the moment is simply lying around and doing nothing in particular.

4 MONDAY
Moon Age Day 14   Moon Sign Gemini

Now that the Sun is in your solar second house you might have the chance to take better control of the financial circumstances governing your life. This enables you to make more progress in money matters than you might have expected. Someone from the past could be paying you a call before long.

5 TUESDAY
Moon Age Day 15   Moon Sign Gemini

There seems to be a great deal of ego and assertiveness around at the moment and at least some of it is coming from your direction. You could be looking towards a period of very hard work in the near future, and it won't help if you cause problems with the people who can best help you. A little humility now goes a long way.

6 WEDNESDAY
Moon Age Day 16   Moon Sign Cancer

It isn't anything big that is likely to go wrong today, but there might be a few little mistakes that add up to some real frustration. Your best approach is to check and double-check all details and don't embark on anything you don't understand. A more comfortable phase is possible later in the day for most.

7 THURSDAY
Moon Age Day 17   Moon Sign Cancer

With present trends around you would be wise to be slightly more frugal than usual. Perhaps you haven't got everything you need for Christmas yet, whilst at the same time money is short. With a little careful planning you can do what is necessary in terms of gifts whilst spending little and also having fun.

8 FRIDAY
Moon Age Day 18   Moon Sign Cancer

A plan of action is essential in what has potential to be a very competitive world right now. You do have a winning instinct and a desire to get ahead, but not everyone will either like or respect the methods you are having to use to get where you want to be. Some careful explanations may be necessary in certain cases.

9 SATURDAY
Moon Age Day 19   Moon Sign Leo

If you want more physical comforts right now, you may need to enlist the support of loved ones in order to make certain this is possible. Luxury appeals and you won't want to be putting yourself out any more than is strictly necessary. Because you can be so loveable it is likely that you can attract all the attention you desire.

10 SUNDAY *Moon Age Day 20   Moon Sign Leo*

You have scope to take positive action in order to improve your finances around now, and that's a good thing as far as the forthcoming festive season is concerned. Your luck seems to be slightly better, but what matters the most is the effort you put in to get a better deal and to earn more when you need it the most.

11 MONDAY *Moon Age Day 21   Moon Sign Virgo*

The present position of the Moon encourages you to get in touch with familiar people from the past, and you could also be rubbing shoulders with someone quite famous before very long. Don't get hung up on details at work, but spend most of today looking at the bigger picture if you can.

12 TUESDAY *Moon Age Day 22   Moon Sign Virgo*

You can be very generous at the moment and that's a good thing, not least because you tend to get back much more than you give in one way or another. This would be a good time to enter competitions and to test your skill against others. Social trends are particularly interesting and remain so for some time.

13 WEDNESDAY *Moon Age Day 23   Moon Sign Libra*

If private emotional matters are on your mind during the middle of this week, you could be somewhat quieter than would normally be the case. Get up and about early if you really want to get on in a practical sense, and don't stand around waiting for life to become interesting. Do something about it!

14 THURSDAY *Moon Age Day 24   Moon Sign Libra*

You could well have to deal with certain monetary matters and responsibilities at some time round about now. This comes harder because the Moon is presently in your solar twelfth house, inclining you to be quieter than of late. Explaining yourself is possible, but people will probably have to be patient with you today.

15 FRIDAY
Moon Age Day 25   Moon Sign Libra

With the accent now firmly on enjoyable communication, you should really be looking forward to what Christmas has to offer. For many of you the festive season starts right now and you should be getting into the right frame of mind. You would be wise to keep an eye on a family member who might have been out of sorts recently.

16 SATURDAY
Moon Age Day 26   Moon Sign Scorpio

There ought to be every reason to smile when you find out just what Lady Luck has on offer for you. A little effort from you won't hurt, but in a general sense the lunar high is supportive in any case. Those you thought you knew very well might still have what it takes to surprise you in a pleasant way.

17 SUNDAY
Moon Age Day 27   Moon Sign Scorpio

This is the best time of the month for making fresh starts and for getting to grips with issues that you may have shied away from recently. Be bold and determined, and don't worry too much if your own ideas don't necessarily agree with those of people you come into contact with generally. In someone's eyes you are a star now!

18 MONDAY
Moon Age Day 28   Moon Sign Sagittarius

You seem to have lots of ideas at your disposal. Even if eight out of ten of them are not workable, that still leaves two that are worth pursuing. With only a few days left until Christmas actually starts, your mind might travel back to previous times. There are lessons to be learned from the past, but probably not many.

19 TUESDAY
Moon Age Day 29   Moon Sign Sagittarius

This is a good time during which to try your hand at money making and innovative enterprises. Help with these is available if you ask around, and you can persuade others to assist you today. There is a quieter side to your nature that might show later, but in the main you are happy to be in the social mainstream.

20 WEDNESDAY   *Moon Age Day 0   Moon Sign Sagittarius*

There are signs that a friendly word in the right ear might enable you to settle a personal issue that has been on your mind. At the same time you can be of significant assistance to colleagues, friends and even your partner. Scorpio is presently at its most co-operative, which helps you to enhance your natural popularity.

21 THURSDAY   *Moon Age Day 1   Moon Sign Capricorn*

You can make the most of a fairly uneventful and easy-going sort of day by laying down those last-minute plans for all that lies ahead of you in the next week or two. Beware of allowing anyone to push you into any sort of scheme that you don't approve of or about which you have severe suspicions.

22 FRIDAY   *Moon Age Day 2   Moon Sign Capricorn*

There is now a good chance to improve your mind in some way, as well as to learn that you are in any case smarter than you might have thought. You love to pit your wits against those of interesting people, whilst at the same time showing a distinctly competitive edge to your Scorpio nature.

23 SATURDAY   *Moon Age Day 3   Moon Sign Aquarius*

Family gatherings ought to be of real interest now, and you might be doing more than most to make these possible. Even if you do not come from a very close family background, you are likely to feel more attached than usual. A sense of 'place' and 'belonging' could well be extremely important to you at present.

24 SUNDAY   *Moon Age Day 4   Moon Sign Aquarius*

There may be some very hopeful news on offer with regard to personal concerns and wishes on this Christmas Eve. From a social and romantic point of view it is those things that come like a bolt from the blue that presently offer the most, so you shouldn't be either upset or worried if you have to change your mind at the last minute.

25 MONDAY   *Moon Age Day 5   Moon Sign Pisces*

If Christmas Day doesn't bring you your heart's desire, it shouldn't be far away. There are a multitude of good planetary aspects surrounding you at the present time and these should assist you to have a good time. You need to be in the company of people you love in order to make the most of what is on offer.

26 TUESDAY   *Moon Age Day 6   Moon Sign Pisces*

If daily life is subject to sudden changes, that could mean having to think on your feet a good deal today. Although you might still be comfortable at home, it's possible you will be taking some time out to visit relatives, and the change of scenery could work to your advantage.

27 WEDNESDAY   *Moon Age Day 7   Moon Sign Aries*

Unexpected domestic challenges could come along at any time now. You will probably be expected to sort them out, which may not be easy if there are also disagreements to be dealt with. Scorpio needs to be especially patient at the moment and to show a very loving face to both relatives and friends.

28 THURSDAY   *Moon Age Day 8   Moon Sign Aries*

This is another good time for communicating. Very few of you will be at work at the moment, but those who are can forge a special bond will colleagues. Ignore the winter weather because it's clear that you need some fresh air in your lungs. Those of you who are away for Christmas probably benefit the most.

29 FRIDAY   *Moon Age Day 9   Moon Sign Taurus*

Look out for a sudden and definite drop in your energy levels today. You can blame the lunar low. What would work best would be to sit in your favourite chair and watch some of the old films on television. You respond very positively to luxury at present, but be careful you don't eat too much!

30 SATURDAY   *Moon Age Day 10   Moon Sign Taurus*

There is potentially still less motivation about, but this is the holiday season after all. Taking some time to think about what you want for the New Year could be good, as well as an hour or two simply to chew the fat with family members or your partner. Social trends improve tomorrow, but you may not feel much like partying today.

31 SUNDAY   *Moon Age Day 11   Moon Sign Taurus*

You have scope to get back on form as the day wears on, and to capitalise on new insights into a subject that is currently uppermost in your mind. Not everyone seems to be on the same wavelength, but by the end of the day you should have more energy and can really enjoy what New Year gatherings have to offer.

SCORPIO:
2007 DIARY PAGES

SCORPIO:
2007 IN BRIEF

You may not start the year with zest, but a little care and attention right from the start will sort this. January and February bring blessings you probably didn't expect and see you working towards your objectives. With everything to play for in the romantic stakes you can warm up the coldest two months of the year and you may discover things about friends that will both surprise and delight you.

With the arrival of the early spring, March and April are likely to offer more in the way of concrete progress and should bring you more of what you want in a financial sense. You cannot afford to splash money around but will be more successful in a material sense and could find yourself taking on some new responsibilities. These trends are continued as the summer approaches but your own choices about where you want to go and what you want to do prove to be more important during May and June. Romance seems to be working well for you at this time, though family relationships might turn out to be slightly more strained than you would wish. New friends will occupy at least part of your time during this period.

The high summer will probably bring you closer to your heart's desire than was possible earlier in the year. You will be very good in terms of organising yourself and will be trying to achieve the same objective for others – sometimes to their slight annoyance. All the same you have winning ways and throughout most of July and August you show a positive and attractive face to the world at large. Travel is extremely likely and you may well be undertaking journeys that come as a surprise or which are arranged at the last minute.

Better luck is forecast for September and October, a time when you reflect on things more and show greater determination in a professional and practical sense. People you don't see too often make a return appearance and you may also undertake a journey that has been planned for quite a time. Confidence remains high and as the Sun gets closer to your part of the zodiac you jump at any chance to get ahead both professionally and personally.

The last two months of the year, November and December, are likely to be a whirl of activity and offer you new starts, more sporting activities and better creative potential. Your thoughts about Christmas are turned into hard and fast realities and you will work hard to offer everyone you encounter a good time. There is likely to be a good deal of nostalgia around, but the very end of the year could be marked with ambitious new plans and a strong sense of co-operation.

January 2007

1 MONDAY
Moon Age Day 13   Moon Sign Gemini

Look out for the chance to make this a very good start to the year. With everything to play for in a personal sense you should be in a very good frame of mind when it comes to romance. Routines are best avoided whilst you get your head round the implications of a brand new year that lies ahead.

2 TUESDAY
Moon Age Day 14   Moon Sign Gemini

If you are back at work today you could be making a sort of progress that you didn't really expect. You attitude generally seems to be very positive and you have what it takes to bring others round to your particular point of view. Some Scorpios will already be planning a 2007 adventure.

3 WEDNESDAY
Moon Age Day 15   Moon Sign Cancer

There could be more social invitations around today than you could possibly have time for. There are signs that you may be sick of celebrating and simply want to get on with the more practical aspects of life. All the same it is important to be diplomatic, because you would not wish to offer any sort of offence to others.

4 THURSDAY
Moon Age Day 16   Moon Sign Cancer

The things you encounter in life generally come along to remind you that you need to bend with the wind. Scorpio can sometimes take a very rigid view of life and that may not serve you under present planetary trends. You have what it takes to make romance burn brightly later in the day.

5 FRIDAY
Moon Age Day 17   Moon Sign Leo

If you intend to be noticed today, you should be doing everything you can to shine out in company. It might be just as well to remember that pride can sometimes go before a fall and also to bear in mind that if you are setting yourself up to be watched, you could be laughed at when things go slightly wrong.

6 SATURDAY
Moon Age Day 18   Moon Sign Leo

Make the most of any personalities who enter your life this weekend by being in the right state of mind to respond in kind. Your popularity is potentially high and you should still be willing to put yourself out on a limb in order to be noticed. Activities that involve family members could prove to be the most rewarding.

7 SUNDAY
Moon Age Day 19   Moon Sign Virgo

You continue to have good ideas, and even if not all of these are based in sound practical reason you can get enough from them to move forward. Actions may not be very likely on a Sunday, at least not in any practical or professional sense. All the more reason to plan rather than do.

8 MONDAY
Moon Age Day 20   Moon Sign Virgo

You would be wise to avoid asking too many questions today or you could end up with some answers you don't like. It would be better for the moment to simply keep your counsel and to work on steadily at your own pace. When workaday matters are out of the way, then you can afford to have some fun, though of a more personal nature.

9 TUESDAY
Moon Age Day 21   Moon Sign Virgo

As a direct contrast to yesterday you now have what it takes to be noticed and need not hold back when your opinion is sought. Trends assist you to be a good team player and to work well when in the company of others. Your originality is what really counts at present and it shines through everything.

10 WEDNESDAY　　　*Moon Age Day 22　Moon Sign Libra*

Actions taken today can have a profound bearing on what happens further down the road, so you do need to be careful over decisions. Even if something you have been wanting for a while now becomes available, there is a strong possibility that you may have changed your mind.

11 THURSDAY　　　*Moon Age Day 23　Moon Sign Libra*

Why not have a quieter sort of day whilst the Moon passes through your solar twelfth house? You may not want to make the running but you can plan ahead because there are some very positive days to come. Romantic overtures could be on offer by the evening and you can lay down plans for the weekend.

12 FRIDAY　　　*Moon Age Day 24　Moon Sign Scorpio*

The green light for action is now on and the things you do today can have repercussions for some time to come. Don't wait to be asked. It is important to grab any initiative and to make it work for you. There are times when Scorpio hides in the shadows, but that shouldn't be the case at the moment.

13 SATURDAY　　　*Moon Age Day 25　Moon Sign Scorpio*

Now is the time to look out for enterprises that are going to make life easier for you later on. Your capacity for work at present is extremely good and you can concentrate for long periods. At the same time it's worth ringing the changes because not everything about today is related to work.

14 SUNDAY　　　*Moon Age Day 26　Moon Sign Scorpio*

For the third day in a row you have scope to gamble and to keep a very high profile when in company. Those who consider you to be a quiet person could well be in for a surprise right now and you should find ways to make the weekend your own. Helping out friends is an option around this time.

15 MONDAY   *Moon Age Day 27   Moon Sign Sagittarius*

There are some good ideas around at the beginning of this week for improving your financial situation. It's worth remembering though that not all the glistens is gold. Your interests are best served if you view all communications with a little scepticism.

16 TUESDAY   *Moon Age Day 28   Moon Sign Sagittarius*

Trends assist you to make your romantic life interesting this week and you could even be able to attract attention from fairly unexpected directions. If someone you don't see very often makes an appearance in your life again, they may well bring with them strong memories of past events.

17 WEDNESDAY   *Moon Age Day 29   Moon Sign Capricorn*

Make use of any positive edge you have over competitors and push your luck at work, even though you might sometimes be slightly lacking in real confidence. It isn't the way you feel that matters but how others perceive you. Why not make a special fuss of a family member who has achieved an important objective?

18 THURSDAY   *Moon Age Day 0   Moon Sign Capricorn*

Scorpio people have what it takes to be especially charming at the moment and to get almost anything they want simply by asking in the right way. Others could find you fascinating to be around, and the very depth of your nature is part of what attracts them. The time is right to play on your natural mystery for all you are worth.

19 FRIDAY   *Moon Age Day 1   Moon Sign Aquarius*

If people at home seem to be keeping you on your toes now, they may well cause you the odd worry by the way they behave. At work you can be efficient and well able to keep many different balls in the air at the same time. Plan now for an action-packed Saturday, maybe thinking in terms of a shopping spree.

20 SATURDAY   *Moon Age Day 2   Moon Sign Aquarius*

Today responds best if you get out of the house and find different ways to keep your mind occupied. Your only enemy right now is potential boredom, and especially so if you can't get your partner or family members motivated. You might have to go it alone in some situations if you really want to motor.

21 SUNDAY   *Moon Age Day 3   Moon Sign Aquarius*

Getting onto the next objective is what matters under present planetary trends and you do have what it takes to think in a big and expansive way. Once again the only thing that holds you back is the unwillingness of others to play ball. By the evening you may decide the time is right to speak your mind romantically.

22 MONDAY   *Moon Age Day 4   Moon Sign Pisces*

Personal attachments can be rather intense, though there is nothing specifically unusual about that in the life of the average Scorpio. You have everything to play for in a practical sense, and might well find ways today to get on the right side of a superior. You can extend your charm to social encounters too.

23 TUESDAY   *Moon Age Day 5   Moon Sign Pisces*

With less intensity about now, you can afford to be approaching life in a more casual manner. Social trends look especially good and it is when you are associated with groups of people that the greatest joys become available. It's worth taking the time out to explain your present thinking to family members.

24 WEDNESDAY   *Moon Age Day 6   Moon Sign Aries*

There could be a definite peak on offer in your career fortunes around now, together with a greater sense of urgency regarding anything that has been on the back burner for a while. Getting to grips with domestic chores can be tedious, which is why you may decide to leave as many of them as you can to others.

25 THURSDAY
Moon Age Day 7   Moon Sign Aries

A change of scenery at some time today can work wonders, the more so because the lunar low is just around the corner. This is the time of the month when the Moon occupies your opposite zodiac sign. Push hard for your objectives today, in the knowledge that achieving them may not be as easy tomorrow.

26 FRIDAY
Moon Age Day 8   Moon Sign Taurus

It may be harder to get things to go the way you wish for today and tomorrow. All the more reason to watch and wait, and to let others take the strain. You could be in a very contemplative frame of mind and may well be showing all the depth that is typical of your zodiac sign. This is not a good time to gamble.

27 SATURDAY
Moon Age Day 9   Moon Sign Taurus

Don't be surprised if you still cannot make the progress you would wish. If nothing can be done, the best thing to do is nothing and since this is a very short interlude, it won't do you any harm at all to take a rest. Routines are easily dealt with and there is something quite comforting about them now.

28 SUNDAY
Moon Age Day 10   Moon Sign Gemini

Trends improve overnight and the lunar low passes out of the way. You do have greater incentives today, but since this is a Sunday you are unlikely to promote any changes of a professional nature. Enjoying yourself in the company of those you love might seem very attractive.

29 MONDAY
Moon Age Day 11   Moon Sign Gemini

You can persuade friends to be very supportive and stimulating at the start of this new working week. Mixing business with pleasure should be easy enough and you can find joy in situations that might have seemed tedious before. Any urgent requests from friends are best addressed quickly.

30 TUESDAY   *Moon Age Day 12   Moon Sign Cancer*

Trends encourage you to avoid becoming involved in the same old things today and wherever possible to get some variety into your life. Even if the weather outside is not very good, you do need a change of scenery. It would be best to pick somewhere warm, but a place where your intellect is stimulated.

31 WEDNESDAY   *Moon Age Day 13   Moon Sign Cancer*

Avoid jobs today that mean you have to deal with boring routines. It would be all too easy at the moment to become bogged down by detail and red tape. Be prepared to approach new situations with a sense of purpose and to tell yourself that you are equal to just about any task, just as long as it really interests you.

February

2007

1 THURSDAY
Moon Age Day 14   Moon Sign Leo

Once again your powers are in the ascendancy and you have what it takes to get ahead. This is a good way to start a new month and you should be brimming with enthusiasm. You have what it takes to retain your confidence, even if your ideas are being questioned by those around you.

2 FRIDAY
Moon Age Day 15   Moon Sign Leo

The focus is on greater financial security, and you could well be looking at various options today. In co-operation with family members and in particular your partner you have an opportunity to firm up family finances, and could well be struck by one or two really good ideas.

3 SATURDAY
Moon Age Day 16   Moon Sign Leo

There are signs that the pursuit of happiness and romantic magic is what drives you this weekend. You can show yourself to be inspirational and very interesting to be around. Even if not all the attention that comes your way is exactly welcome, that's part of the price of being so magnetic and attractive.

4 SUNDAY
Moon Age Day 17   Moon Sign Virgo

Mental activities are now highlighted and you can afford to stretch yourself in some way. Everything from a sudoku to a new and fiendishly difficult computer game could captivate you, and you won't give in until you succeed. It's worth keeping a strong sense of proportion over any disputes in your family.

5 MONDAY　　　　*Moon Age Day 18　Moon Sign Virgo*

Your social life could bring some surprises today. It is possible that you will be learning something about a friend about which you had no idea, and that this could come as a very definite surprise. You may decide to use your current heightened creativity to make changes in your living space.

6 TUESDAY　　　　*Moon Age Day 19　Moon Sign Virgo*

Stand by for a time of some inner reflection. Planets conspire to assist you to be far more introspective. Since you are often given to such periods it is possible that no one will really notice the difference. Scorpio is certainly not miserable at present, though you may think about the past much more than usual.

7 WEDNESDAY　　　*Moon Age Day 20　Moon Sign Libra*

The Sun in your solar fourth house offers a period of benefits as far as your domestic life is concerned. All the more reason to turn your attention towards family members and to do whatever you can to support loved ones. At work you may now be less inclined to push yourself forward.

8 THURSDAY　　　*Moon Age Day 21　Moon Sign Libra*

If you try hard to emphasise your personality at the moment you could notice how much others rally to support you. However, the Moon is now in your solar twelfth house so there is still a part of you that wishes to remain quiet. You can change things significantly by tomorrow.

9 FRIDAY　　　　*Moon Age Day 22　Moon Sign Scorpio*

Success should now be there for the taking as a direct result of your own efforts. You have the ability to get major initiatives to go your way, and to persuade colleagues and friends to help you out. Life may be frenetic during the lunar high, but it is also very interesting.

10 SATURDAY *Moon Age Day 23   Moon Sign Scorpio*

Your originality is heightened now and you can move quickly towards specific targets in your life as a whole. Try to keep some major ambitions on the boil and be sure to get involved in new projects. Getting to where you want to be should be a piece of cake across this weekend.

11 SUNDAY *Moon Age Day 24   Moon Sign Scorpio*

Although the lunar high is still around, it's possible that your finances may be stretched at the moment. Even if you decide to keep a lock on your purse or wallet, at the same time you should realise that there are moments when it is sensible to speculate in order to accumulate later.

12 MONDAY *Moon Age Day 25   Moon Sign Sagittarius*

Mercury is in a useful position when it comes to romantic liaisons of any sort. You have just the right words to sweep someone important off their feet and you shouldn't be in the least fazed by the attention that you can attract in your direction. Small aches and pains are possible under other planetary trends.

13 TUESDAY *Moon Age Day 26   Moon Sign Sagittarius*

There are signs that coming to a final decision regarding a deeply personal matter may prove to be quite important today. You need to be very sure of yourself and should not make decisions without serious thought. Nevertheless you can't live your life backwards and can afford to commit yourself to certain and very specific changes.

14 WEDNESDAY ☿ *Moon Age Day 27   Moon Sign Capricorn*

What is highlighted at the moment is your marked ability to communicate your ideas and opinions to anyone who is willing to listen. Confidence remains potentially high, even if you are occasionally shaking in your shoes when confronted by anyone you see as being very important.

15 THURSDAY ☿ *Moon Age Day 28   Moon Sign Capricorn*

Attracting the good things in life should not be too difficult today and is partly down to the very real consideration of those around you. If you can encourage colleagues to be especially attentive, they may take some pressure from you in a work sense. Make the most of favours repaid by others.

16 FRIDAY ☿ *Moon Age Day 0   Moon Sign Aquarius*

Engaging in heartfelt discussions is something that comes as second nature ahead of the weekend. This is especially true in the case of family members and also your life partner. Scorpio people who have been looking for love might be well advised to concentrate their efforts now and to keep their eyes open.

17 SATURDAY ☿ *Moon Age Day 1   Moon Sign Aquarius*

You seem to be very assertive today, though 'seem' is probably the operative word. It doesn't matter how lacking you might be in confidence just as long as you don't show the fact. Persuading others is within your power, and you can make full use of any help that is on offer.

18 SUNDAY ☿ *Moon Age Day 2   Moon Sign Pisces*

Pleasant social opportuities seem to be on the increase. Although it is still early in the year chances are that you are noticing the first signs of nature waking from her winter sleep. A little fresh air could do you the world of good, so why not get out into a garden and look for the snowdrops and crocuses?

19 MONDAY ☿ *Moon Age Day 3   Moon Sign Pisces*

The focus at the start of this week is not likely to be on practical matters but rather in the direction of intimate attachments. Anything to do with your home is also to the fore, so it could be rather difficult committing yourself fully to work or even certain social events.

20 TUESDAY ☿ *Moon Age Day 4 Moon Sign Aries*

You may need to discipline yourself more today if you are to get through a mountain of work that seems to stand in front of you. When moving this heap your best approach is to attack it one stone at a time. The less complicated you make life, the greater can be your success. Slow and steady wins the Scorpio race.

21 WEDNESDAY ☿ *Moon Age Day 5 Moon Sign Aries*

The Sun is now in your solar fifth house, where it will remain for the next month or so. This brings a period during which you can afford to show much greater optimism than has been the case recently. This is especially true in a romantic sense, so if there is someone you want to sweep off their feet, now is the time to grab a brush!

22 THURSDAY ☿ *Moon Age Day 6 Moon Sign Taurus*

It might be best not to expect too much of life today or tomorrow. The Moon is in Taurus, your opposite zodiac sign, and it brings with it the lunar low. It's worth allowing others to take most of the strain whilst you stop and watch life go by. It won't do you any harm at all to stand in the background a little.

23 FRIDAY ☿ *Moon Age Day 7 Moon Sign Taurus*

You are in the midst of a lull patch and your best option is to get used to the idea. If you push too hard you could well find that jobs have to be done time and again. A time to watch and wait, whilst planning for a much more productive period that lies just around the corner. Also avoid tackling more than one job at once.

24 SATURDAY ☿ *Moon Age Day 8 Moon Sign Gemini*

Romance can be strengthened at the moment and this is definitely the right time to tell someone exactly how you feel. Relaxation is advisable in all your approaches because if you get yourself uptight you could stutter and stumble. Support on important issues can be obtained from friends.

25 SUNDAY ☿ *Moon Age Day 9* *Moon Sign Gemini*

There could be something missing today, though it might be hard to put your finger upon what that might be. It's time to ask a few leading questions and to make a diligent search for the missing components of your life. Be prepared to spend at least part of today doing something that is not remotely important but quite interesting.

26 MONDAY ☿ *Moon Age Day 10* *Moon Sign Gemini*

You open a new week with a very hectic period and a time in which it may well be difficult to achieve everything that is expected of you. The same advice that has been around for most of this month remains in place. Do one thing at once and when it is achieved move onto the next task.

27 TUESDAY ☿ *Moon Age Day 11* *Moon Sign Cancer*

Though your domestic life is well highlighted under present planetary trends, you could be slightly too sensitive and emotional for your own good. Scorpio may be easily brought to tears right now, even if you have little or nothing to cry about. It's possible that thoughts about the past are entering your mind.

28 WEDNESDAY ☿ *Moon Age Day 12* *Moon Sign Cancer*

You can focus on making significant changes in your employment status around this time. Maybe you are looking for an increase in pay or else the chance to take on new responsibilities. Whatever you are looking for, a good heart-to-heart with someone who is in charge could be the way forward under present trends.

2007

1 THURSDAY *Moon Age Day 13   Moon Sign Leo*

You have scope to open the new month on a positive note and to continue to focus on your work. Move slowly ahead with your chosen objectives but don't ignore the very real common sense of friends, some of whom may be trying to tell you things you don't necessarily want to hear.

2 FRIDAY *Moon Age Day 14   Moon Sign Leo*

Trends encourage you to pay special attention to the feelings of others, especially members of your family. It could be that you have been ignoring someone recently, even if this was accidental. Just a few words in the right place could make all the difference, and could enable you to gain an important ally when it matters the most.

3 SATURDAY *Moon Age Day 15   Moon Sign Virgo*

There seem to be things happening in the outside world that could offer you plenty of stimulation, even if the pressures of your life generally prevent you from becoming quite as committed as you might wish. Routines are for the birds this weekend, especially if you decide to do what takes your fancy.

4 SUNDAY *Moon Age Day 16   Moon Sign Virgo*

You want to be appreciated but it's possible that in some quarters at least you are being ignored. Is this really the case? Perhaps you are brooding in a corner instead of making yourself known. It's time to speak out and to show everyone just how intelligent and erudite you can be.

5 MONDAY ☿ *Moon Age Day 17 Moon Sign Virgo*

Venus is in your solar sixth house and this ought to be good for all aspects associated with work. You will be in a good position to explain yourself to colleagues and superiors, whilst at the same time shining out like a beacon in terms of your performance. New input and new information count at present.

6 TUESDAY ☿ *Moon Age Day 18 Moon Sign Libra*

Today your intuitive powers are highlighted, and it would be a very good person who managed to pull the wool over your eyes. You have what it takes to offer advice to friends, and to keep relationships settled and happy. Stand by for a few conclusions on your part that baffle everyone.

7 WEDNESDAY ☿ *Moon Age Day 19 Moon Sign Libra*

There could be plenty of nostalgia in the air at present and tendency on your part to spend almost as much time in the past as in the present. There is not a lot to be gained from this way of being, but it is part of what makes all Water sign individuals tick. Why not make use of the trend by contacting someone from the past?

8 THURSDAY ☿ *Moon Age Day 20 Moon Sign Scorpio*

Today your gift is your enthusiasm. Your level of optimism is high and you shouldn't let much stand in your way. With the lunar high also comes the chance of better luck, which you should be pushing for all you are worth. You will also be far more committed to the future than has been the case for a few days.

9 FRIDAY *Moon Age Day 21 Moon Sign Scorpio*

Taking the odd risk could allow you to achieve significant success and you shouldn't be in the least fazed by having to think on your feet. Arrange outings for this time and make use of the fact that the weather is improving slightly and the nights are getting longer. You can persuade relatives to be especially accommodating.

10 SATURDAY *Moon Age Day 22 Moon Sign Scorpio*

For the third day in a row you have what it takes to be dynamic and go-getting. Don't be in the least surprised if you start to run out of steam in the afternoon, particularly if you have been keeping up a pace that cannot be maintained indefinitely. A day to give some thought to family outings that include everyone.

11 SUNDAY *Moon Age Day 23 Moon Sign Sagittarius*

This is still a good time to take centre stage. It's possible that your actions are now slightly more considered and that you won't take the risks that were evident earlier in the week but you are willing to listen and that's what really counts. Your present mixture of ego and modesty is a very potent one.

12 MONDAY *Moon Age Day 24 Moon Sign Sagittarius*

Today could be a very busy time, especially at work. Scorpio people who have been looking for a new job would be wise to keep their eyes open at the moment, and you show a strong ability to adapt to prevailing circumstances. Even if there are demands on your time, it is important to leave moments for socialising.

13 TUESDAY *Moon Age Day 25 Moon Sign Capricorn*

The Moon in your solar third house imparts a restless mind and encourages you to wonder about things that you previously assumed were settled. Maybe you are searching too deeply within yourself and would do better to settle down. There are signs that somewhere within you is a sort of discontent.

14 WEDNESDAY *Moon Age Day 26 Moon Sign Capricorn*

You can now take advantage of a smoother period and a time during which you are able to fulfil your obligations generally. Social trends are favourable and there are happy moments to be had in the company of friends. You can be particularly good when involved in group activities that demand co-operation.

15 THURSDAY   *Moon Age Day 27   Moon Sign Capricorn*

The focus is on reconciling family difficulties or at least acting as an honest broker when it comes to solving problems elsewhere. People will trust you to take a neutral point of view and that is what you must seek to do under present trends. Mixing business with pleasure shouldn't be hard with the Moon in your solar fourth house.

16 FRIDAY   *Moon Age Day 28   Moon Sign Aquarius*

The source of your energy at the moment seems to be your desire to entertain others. This could be the most selfless interlude during March, particularly if you are doing a lot for the world at large. Don't think that the attention you pay to everyone else goes unnoticed. On the contrary, you might be being closely watched.

17 SATURDAY   *Moon Age Day 29   Moon Sign Aquarius*

Your love of life can be very impressive and offers you a time of high enthusiasm. The weekend should offer ample opportunity for having a good time, perhaps in the company of your partner or other family members. Your best areas are love and leisure pursuits.

18 SUNDAY   *Moon Age Day 0   Moon Sign Pisces*

There is a strong desire to make changes. Whether this is a purely astrological phenomenon is hard to say. It might also be down to the nature of the changing year. Now would be a very good time to plan alterations to your abode, even if you decide not to actually implement them for a month or two.

19 MONDAY   *Moon Age Day 1   Moon Sign Pisces*

You would be best off dealing quietly with practical matters today. Leave alone any desire to push forward too hard because it's possible you will only come up against stumbling blocks. Don't be afraid to enlist the support of friends for projects that are at the forefront of your mind, and to enjoy the social trends that look especially good.

20 TUESDAY · Moon Age Day 2 · Moon Sign Aries

Trends now encourage a strong love of life and in particular a fondness for romantic matters. You may be proving to be a good matchmaker and at the same time have a chance to pep up your own love life. A day to stay away from pointless and boring routines, because these will only sap your energy.

21 WEDNESDAY · Moon Age Day 3 · Moon Sign Aries

The pressures seem to mount up today but if you tell yourself that this is little more than an illusion and is down to the lunar low, you can ensure that all is well. You can't expect to get your heart's desire at the moment, but there is nothing to prevent you from planning and putting things in place.

22 THURSDAY · Moon Age Day 4 · Moon Sign Taurus

If practical goals and objectives come up against unexpected problems, you will have to deal with these as and when they arise. Keep an open mind but be willing to shelve certain ambitions for the moment. If you simply plug away at life in your usual way, you can make sure the difficulties soon pass.

23 FRIDAY · Moon Age Day 5 · Moon Sign Taurus

It is now time to emphasise your own practical ideas and to show your enthusiasm in everything you do. If you can put your business head on you should do well in situations that require a good deal of native wit. People could well marvel at your ability to handle several different tasks at the same time.

24 SATURDAY · Moon Age Day 6 · Moon Sign Gemini

If you are accused of being selfish and of putting your own interests ahead of those of others, you need to look carefully at what is being said. Chances are that these assertions are totally wrong and it may be necessary to initiate a serious heart-to-heart to clear the air properly.

25 SUNDAY   *Moon Age Day 7   Moon Sign Gemini*

The search is on for greater personal freedom, and this may not go
down well with everyone. Female Scorpios especially may feel their
horizons to be clouded by responsibility, and it appears that the
Scorpion is about to break out. This happens occasionally, and is
nothing especially unusual for you.

26 MONDAY   *Moon Age Day 8   Moon Sign Cancer*

Current plans and objectives that are close to your heart should be
pursued for all you are worth at the start of this new working week.
These are likely to be predominantly practical in nature and may
also involve how money is spent. You have what it takes to
strengthen your general level of good luck now.

27 TUESDAY   *Moon Age Day 9   Moon Sign Cancer*

You probably won't thrive on being alone at the moment. Venus is
in your solar seventh house and that means you need support if you
are to really enjoy yourself. It's worth sticking with like-minded
people and especially with friends you have known for a long time.
A breath of fresh air at some stage now would do you no end of
good.

28 WEDNESDAY   *Moon Age Day 10   Moon Sign Leo*

At home the planet Mars encourages assertiveness and whether or
not you are head of the household you may well behave as if you
are. You need to deal with emotional matters firmly and fairly and
should take on board the considered opinions of everyone, no
matter how young they may be.

29 THURSDAY   *Moon Age Day 11   Moon Sign Leo*

New information that you can obtain today could assist you to get
ahead positively at work. There is much about today that works best
on a practical level, though you are showing signs of entering a
much more emotional and romantic period too. The wheels of
progress grind on, and you may well be operating them!

30 FRIDAY
Moon Age Day 12   Moon Sign Leo

There is help waiting in the wings and all you have to do is to ask for it. The only problem here is that you are naturally very independently minded and don't take kindly to having to demean yourself in any way. Sometimes your ego is too strong for your own good, and this could be such a time.

31 SATURDAY
Moon Age Day 13   Moon Sign Virgo

Love life and relationships generally could prove to be very rewarding this weekend. You are able to restore your faith in human nature regarding recent issues and at the same time you know exactly how to entertain others. You can get people to marvel at your staying power in almost any situation.

April

2007

1 SUNDAY
Moon Age Day 14   Moon Sign Virgo

The fun side of your nature is what really counts on this Sunday. The weather is improving and there should be a touch of spring in the air. This is something that shouldn't pass you by as you seek to broaden your horizons and in particular to travel. Short or long journeys are well highlighted now.

2 MONDAY
Moon Age Day 15   Moon Sign Libra

It might be far too easy to put your faith in the wrong people at the start of this week. Before you commit yourself to anything, your best approach would be to look at situations very carefully and then only proceed with caution. In particular, you would be wise to hang on to money until later in the week.

3 TUESDAY
Moon Age Day 16   Moon Sign Libra

Now you have a chance to show a natural talent for communicating in terms of romantic matters. You can pep up an existing relationship or get a new one started. With everything to play for in a financial sense, you may also be able to make monetary gains. When it comes to charm and persuasion, you can be top of the class.

4 WEDNESDAY
Moon Age Day 17   Moon Sign Libra

Favourable results can be achieved through persistence and determination, two qualities that you have in abundance. Even the presence of the Moon in your solar twelfth house need do little to curb your enthusiasm, though there may be quieter moments later in the day – that is if you can find time for them!

5 THURSDAY   *Moon Age Day 18*   *Moon Sign Scorpio*

The more ambitious you are with regard to dreams and schemes, the more likely it is that you can make them turn out the way you would wish. Don't take no for an answer when you know you have it within you to talk people round, and be certain to speak to everyone you encounter. Your charm is now way off the scale.

6 FRIDAY   *Moon Age Day 19*   *Moon Sign Scorpio*

A period of creative inspiration is now at hand, and if you don't want to waste a moment of it you need to get cracking very early in the day. Trends offer you plenty of energy and the ability to keep going long after others fall by the wayside. Scorpio can be especially warm at the moment and has scope to show the fact in romantic clinches.

7 SATURDAY   *Moon Age Day 20*   *Moon Sign Sagittarius*

Your strength lies in remaining essentially self-confident and not falling prey to negative thinking, even if those around you seem to be doing so all the time. There is still a great deal of drive within you and you shouldn't stop until you get where you want to be. It's worth saving some time later in the day for simply having fun.

8 SUNDAY   *Moon Age Day 21*   *Moon Sign Sagittarius*

Beneficial material trends are evident, and making financial decisions at this time is recommended. One option is to get together with family members and decide now about alterations you wish to make at home. The advancing year lies in front of you and the future looks like an exciting path winding over the next horizon.

9 MONDAY   *Moon Age Day 22*   *Moon Sign Sagittarius*

There could be a high spot in the romantic sphere this week and it probably starts today. Venus is in your solar seventh house, a sure sign that you are in a position to look for love. You might also be keen to see new places, and locations that carry a specific interest could be featured more than most.

10 TUESDAY *Moon Age Day 23 Moon Sign Capricorn*

You could be working harder than ever right now. If there is something you really want to achieve, you have all the staying power necessary to go out and get it. Routines will seem to be quite a bore, and instead the focus is on spontaneous actions. Why not enlist the specific help of an expert?

11 WEDNESDAY *Moon Age Day 24 Moon Sign Capricorn*

This is another auspicious period in terms of your work and you can afford to put plenty of energy in that direction. If there is any time to spare you might be thinking about a spring-clean and will want to chase away the last cobwebs of winter in order to allow the new light of spring to penetrate you home.

12 THURSDAY *Moon Age Day 25 Moon Sign Aquarius*

The planet of love is still affecting personal relationships and it gives you every incentive to solidify an attachment. For those of you who are involved in a long-term relationship there is the possibility for you to turn up the heat and to make sure you are cherishing that old flame.

13 FRIDAY *Moon Age Day 26 Moon Sign Aquarius*

This is a period during which there are changes being made to your goals and intentions. If there is any alteration that needs making at work, this is the best time to be thinking about it. You seem to be able to persuade superiors and even colleagues to give you an important leg up.

14 SATURDAY *Moon Age Day 27 Moon Sign Pisces*

Everyone knows how important it is to make a favourable impression and you are certainly not in the dark about that. Now is the time to seek out those who have the most power to make things happen for you and give them a nudge. If you don't ask, you will never know, and even a refusal means people are considering your requests.

15 SUNDAY
Moon Age Day 28   Moon Sign Pisces

Expanding your horizons has rarely been easier. Today responds best if you move forward one step at a time and ensure that those around you are quite familiar with your intentions. Taking time out to be with friends would be no bad thing. Even if this is a busy Sunday, you must find time for yourself.

16 MONDAY
Moon Age Day 29   Moon Sign Aries

You can now put the finishing touches to changes that started as early as Monday of last week. Balancing your own needs with those of the world at large might not be all that easy but it is essential. Younger family members in particular might give you great cause to be proud of them.

17 TUESDAY
Moon Age Day 0   Moon Sign Aries

This fairly hectic phase of your life suggests that you are in the best possible position to help yourself in a career sense. You can make the most of a high-profile period and a time during which your every action is being carefully watched. It's time to be on your best behaviour and to pass around a few compliments.

18 WEDNESDAY
Moon Age Day 1   Moon Sign Taurus

There could be some difficulties associated with any area of life, and for this you can thank the lunar low. Pushing forward might be a waste of time and you would be best advised to take a little break from hard graft. Stand and watch the flowers grow – you can gather new ideas from even this pastime.

19 THURSDAY
Moon Age Day 2   Moon Sign Taurus

Your current aims and objectives could easily seem to be out of proportion with what you know about reality, but this has much more to do with your present state of mind than any practical situation. You needn't make changes or slacken the general pressure for progress – just wait until tomorrow and then look again.

20 FRIDAY
Moon Age Day 3   Moon Sign Gemini

Improved health and an easier path towards career objectives are there for the taking with the passing of the lunar low. The Sun is now in your solar seventh house, making this a very positive time during which to apply greater self-discipline. Something you once thought impossible could be achieved any day.

21 SATURDAY
Moon Age Day 4   Moon Sign Gemini

If you let yourself become preoccupied in trying to get to the root of a personal issue, this is likely to make it difficult to concentrate on other matters. Nevertheless you would benefit from a change of scenery and need the chance to spread your wings in some way. Even a trip into town to do some shopping might be good.

22 SUNDAY
Moon Age Day 5   Moon Sign Cancer

This is probably the best period of the month as far as plain and simple friendship is concerned. Don't hold back when it comes to telling your pals how much they mean to you and spend as much time in their company as you can. If you get tired doing one task, you can afford to take a break and think about something else.

23 MONDAY
Moon Age Day 6   Moon Sign Cancer

Trends suggest a strong need to do your own thing this week, even if that goes against the grain as far as others are concerned. You probably won't get very far if you are living some sort of lie, and the truth of your own feelings is likely to catch up with you eventually. You might even decide it is time to be a little blunt.

24 TUESDAY
Moon Age Day 7   Moon Sign Leo

With Mars now in your solar fifth house it is possible for you to make this a period of intense recreation. This might not be entirely convenient, particularly if you are very busy at the moment, but there may be little you can do about the situation. You need diversions and will be bored if you don't get them.

25 WEDNESDAY   *Moon Age Day 8   Moon Sign Leo*

There may now be a fresh opportunity to get ahead in something that is of great importance to you. The window is not wide but you can probably make headway during the middle part of today. By the late afternoon it's worth turning your thoughts more in the direction of home-based realities.

26 THURSDAY   *Moon Age Day 9   Moon Sign Leo*

Today offers an opportunity to meet people who could prove to be very accommodating and as friendly as can be. Although this may not be entirely surprising in the main, it could be in one or two cases. You may even be able to get on well with someone you previously thought disliked you.

27 FRIDAY   *Moon Age Day 10   Moon Sign Virgo*

There are pleasant activities to be looked at as the working week draws to a close. Scorpio is coming out of its winter shell and you should be able to discover hidden depths within your own nature. Although you might not be the noisiest person around, you do have plenty to say!

28 SATURDAY   *Moon Age Day 11   Moon Sign Virgo*

In your dealings with others this weekend you can show yourself to be diplomatic and well able to exercise your social skills. Refined and even elevated in your approach, you can make sure that everyone wants to know you better. Feathering your own nest for the future is entirely possible under such trends as these.

29 SUNDAY   *Moon Age Day 12   Moon Sign Libra*

Scorpio is sometimes accused of being a little selfish, but that is probably not something that can be levelled at you today. Almost everything you do can be for the benefit of others, especially if you decide to put your own needs firmly in a cupboard. This is a very good time to prove what you are really like.

30 MONDAY

Moon Age Day 13   Moon Sign Libra

The Sun in your solar seventh house points to personal relationships and highlights the way you feel about them. Even if you remain quite busy in a practical sense, you have what it takes to find the necessary moments to tell people how much they mean to you. You have no idea how important this is likely to be.

May

2007

1 TUESDAY
Moon Age Day 14   Moon Sign Libra

A slightly quieter day precedes the lunar high, which comes along tomorrow. In the meantime you would be wise to consolidate and to lay in preparations for activity. Instead of taking on anything new today, why not simply clear the decks for action? Someone you don't see very often could be making a return visit to your life.

2 WEDNESDAY
Moon Age Day 15   Moon Sign Scorpio

Today it seems as though nothing is impossible. Trends assist you to be in the best frame of mind for ages and to be more than willing to put yourself out in any way that seems necessary. What you should be seeking is personal advancement, something that is entirely possible whilst the lunar high is around.

3 THURSDAY
Moon Age Day 16   Moon Sign Scorpio

Now your attempts at making significant headway could well be paying dividends. Your popularity has potential to be off the scale and you can afford to show a greater sense of determination than has been present for ages. If you make the most of today, things have the definite potential to turn out a great deal better than you may have expected.

4 FRIDAY
Moon Age Day 17   Moon Sign Sagittarius

A smooth period is on offer, and one during which your closest attachments are of supreme importance. Advertising your abilities won't do you any harm, especially in any situation that involves work. A day to remain committed to personal progress at every level and to show your cheerfulness.

5 SATURDAY   *Moon Age Day 18   Moon Sign Sagittarius*

In terms of balance it seems as though you can make this a very good day. It might almost appear as though events will sort themselves out, such is your present ability to make significant progress. Romance looks especially good and you automatically have the right words to sweep your lover off their feet.

6 SUNDAY   *Moon Age Day 19   Moon Sign Sagittarius*

Be prepared to show a great desire to express yourself and to be as creative as possible. It is entirely likely that you are discovering skills within yourself that you didn't even know you possessed. You can afford to take some time out to explore these new directions because they could prove both interesting and rewarding.

7 MONDAY   *Moon Age Day 20   Moon Sign Capricorn*

Today you have the ability to communicate easily with others and to show great flexibility, which isn't always the case for Scorpio. With a great desire to learn you have a chance to cast your net far and wide in order to amass the necessary information to make your life smoother and to find new ways to help your friends.

8 TUESDAY   *Moon Age Day 21   Moon Sign Capricorn*

You should certainly be more willing now to put others first and to constantly move the goalposts for them. That's fine, but there may be occasions on which you have to think about your own life too. Routines could be a real drag at times now, so why not do your best to avoid them?

9 WEDNESDAY   *Moon Age Day 22   Moon Sign Aquarius*

Today would be a good time for travel, even if these are journeys that are arranged at the very last minute. There are signs that there is plenty of energy available and a desire to break new ground in almost everything you do. Even if there are minor frustrations to be dealt with, you should sort these out easily and without any fuss.

10 THURSDAY *Moon Age Day 23   Moon Sign Aquarius*

The focus on your career that has been so marked in the last week or two tends to be less evident now, allowing you to spend more time thinking about your personal and social life. In a domestic sense this could be a relaxed and quite easy-going period, with new attachments possible for young or young-at-heart Scorpios.

11 FRIDAY *Moon Age Day 24   Moon Sign Pisces*

It's worth being very sensitive to the impression you make on others and treading very carefully in order not to offer offence. The deeper qualities of your nature are definitely present and not everyone will be able to understand that Scorpio intensity. Your best response is to explain yourself if this is possible.

12 SATURDAY *Moon Age Day 25   Moon Sign Pisces*

You enjoy the benefits that come from constant changes of scene and probably won't take at all kindly to being restricted in your movements. The greater the flexibility you show in a general sense, the more you can turn life your way. Communication is well accented under present influences.

13 SUNDAY *Moon Age Day 26   Moon Sign Pisces*

This is a great time for Scorpios to be part of relationships of any kind. Be prepared to get involved in twosomes and to build new bridges with regard to people you haven't necessarily been on good terms with recently. Active and enterprising, you can also show a good deal of discrimination and should know instinctively what looks right.

14 MONDAY *Moon Age Day 27   Moon Sign Aries*

The Moon in your solar sixth house encourages a greater commitment to work and brings a temporary slackening of some of the more social trends that are still present. For the moment you may be dealing with practical matters and may not have the hours necessary to sort out the problems of the world today.

15 TUESDAY   *Moon Age Day 28   Moon Sign Aries*

There could well be all sorts of small pressures around today. These conspire to make it difficult to get ahead. Such is the bearing that the approaching lunar low has on you for the next couple of days, though this doesn't need to be a negative time at all. There are moments during which you can plan ahead, and your vision for the future remains good.

16 WEDNESDAY   *Moon Age Day 29   Moon Sign Taurus*

Any little setbacks today probably occur because your general energies are low. Now is the time to lean on others when you can and seek out those who are more than willing to offer you timely assistance. If you are canny in the way you deal with life, nobody would guess that you are lacking in anything.

17 THURSDAY   *Moon Age Day 0   Moon Sign Taurus*

With the lunar low now receding, you can begin to respond more to a sixth-house Mars. If you want things done exactly your own way, you won't take at all kindly to having others arrange your life. It is possible you will also feel cornered in some way, and that is when the Scorpion is at its most dangerous.

18 FRIDAY   *Moon Age Day 1   Moon Sign Gemini*

What a good day this is for solving problems! Mercury is in your solar eighth house and this supports your ability to speak about the changes you want to make, especially to routines. There is hardly anyone or anything that you can't persuade to respond to your active mind and your penetrating gaze.

19 SATURDAY   *Moon Age Day 2   Moon Sign Gemini*

It is towards the more cultured side of life that trends encourage you to turn for most of this weekend. You will probably avoid anything coarse or vulgar and show a strong intellectual quality, no matter what you decide to do. You might be thinking about a visit to a museum, a stately home or maybe a beautiful garden.

20 SUNDAY
Moon Age Day 3   Moon Sign Cancer

Even if you are now more selective and practical, you still have scope to learn more about your inner mind and the way the world works. This burning curiosity is likely to be around for quite some time, assisting you to search out new ways to look at life. A day to surprise others with kind actions.

21 MONDAY
Moon Age Day 4   Moon Sign Cancer

A great deal of vigour can be put into work projects as a new week gets underway. There should be nobody around who will beat you to the punch regarding matters that specifically interest you, and your capacity for making decisions is better than for some time. Personal attachments may have to wait until late in the day.

22 TUESDAY
Moon Age Day 5   Moon Sign Leo

Now you would be wise to look more carefully at emotional matters, particularly if you have failed to address the issues they bring into your life for a few days. Your tendency recently has been to look at the world as a whole, whereas necessities now suggest you should deal with your partner especially in a very direct sense.

23 WEDNESDAY
Moon Age Day 6   Moon Sign Leo

You could really enjoy exploring the world at the moment and the only slight frustration that may be evident today could be the fact that practical necessities prevent you from doing so. In terms of important decisions you can now afford to hedge your bets whenever possible.

24 THURSDAY
Moon Age Day 7   Moon Sign Virgo

Work developments have potential to give you a rather bumpy ride. Don't be afraid to slow things down to a more manageable pace and allow others to make some of the running. If you put yourself into thinking mode, you have the opportunity to discover that your capacity for looking ahead is as good as it ever gets.

25 FRIDAY   *Moon Age Day 8   Moon Sign Virgo*

A phase of transition is at hand. The Sun has now entered your solar eighth house and for the next month or so it's possible for circumstances to change quite significantly. This can be somewhat disquieting for Scorpio, but probably won't be too bad this time round, particularly if you are making most of the alterations yourself.

26 SATURDAY   *Moon Age Day 9   Moon Sign Virgo*

Newer and warmer relationships can be developed as a result of group activities. You are now at your best when involved with other people and the more insular qualities of Scorpio are less likely to display themselves to the world at large. A day to get into gear regarding a plan that could lead to a long and interesting journey.

27 SUNDAY   *Moon Age Day 10   Moon Sign Libra*

At home there is no task that lies beyond your interest or your capacity to get involved. Trends encourage you to revel in anything new and to look very carefully around you, in order to see what you can do to make your living circumstances more interesting. Offering support to friends would be no bad thing.

28 MONDAY   *Moon Age Day 11   Moon Sign Libra*

Though the focus is on a strong desire to be of assistance, not everyone may be too willing to allow you access to either their plans or their thoughts. You need to be a good deal nosier than would normally be the case if you really want to be in the know, and shouldn't be afraid of turning over many stones throughout today.

29 TUESDAY   *Moon Age Day 12   Moon Sign Scorpio*

You can boost your self-confidence now that the Moon has returned to your own zodiac sign. With everything in place it is now time to move forward progressively and to reap the rewards of some of your past efforts. If there is any frustration about today, it may be because you can't move as quickly as you would wish.

30 WEDNESDAY   *Moon Age Day 13   Moon Sign Scorpio*

You have what it takes to be optimistic, idealistic and inspiring. In short you should be good to have around, and you can use this to increase your general popularity no end. With every possible initiative in place it is difficult to see how you could fail to make a significant advancement or alter your life for the better in a general sense.

31 THURSDAY   *Moon Age Day 14   Moon Sign Scorpio*

Even if you are generous to a fault today, not everyone may be equally giving, and you would be wise to watch out for the possibility that someone is trying to pull the wool over your eyes. Such can be your concentration and your intuition at present that they would have to get up very early in the morning to fool you.

June

2007

1 FRIDAY
Moon Age Day 15   Moon Sign Sagittarius

The first day of June would be a particularly excellent time to take a trip or to plan something exotic with your romantic partner. Any way that you can broaden your mind is grist to the mill under present planetary trends, and you may even decide to use these influences to get on top of a slightly sticky financial matter.

2 SATURDAY
Moon Age Day 16   Moon Sign Sagittarius

There are signs that you may be attracted to someone who is quite unusual in the way they look at life. This is a great time to break free from normal conventions, and Scorpios across the board can now show themselves to be quite revolutionary in their general approach. Rewards can be gained as a result of past efforts.

3 SUNDAY
Moon Age Day 17   Moon Sign Capricorn

It's worth staying as close to loved ones as you can today. There may be a temporary blip in the forward progress you have been making and a tendency for you to feel somewhat insecure. The right words of love coming from the direction of someone special should put you right in no time. Home-based matters are well accented now.

4 MONDAY
Moon Age Day 18   Moon Sign Capricorn

Family matters tend to be very rewarding under present planetary influence. Career developments, however, may need extra care, and it is possible that you will be inclined to make silly mistakes of one sort or another. There could be some financial gains on offer later in the day.

5 TUESDAY
Moon Age Day 19   Moon Sign Aquarius

With Mars, the planet of energy and action, now in your solar sixth house, you can get plans organised and should be able to move forward quite positively on most fronts. You would be wise to avoid getting involved in family rows that are not of your own making, and wherever it proves to be possible, to play the honest broker.

6 WEDNESDAY
Moon Age Day 20   Moon Sign Aquarius

The planet of communication is definitely at work now and offers you the chance to make contact with those who can be most useful to you at this time. At work you can show yourself to be more than capable and could well get yourself singled out for special treatment from superiors.

7 THURSDAY
Moon Age Day 21   Moon Sign Aquarius

A boost to your social life is now available, helping to make this part of the week more than interesting for most Scorpio individuals. Romance is also highlighted, and you can use this interlude to think about ways in which you can make your partner or sweetheart feel more comfortable generally.

8 FRIDAY
Moon Age Day 22   Moon Sign Pisces

Be prepared to show great enthusiasm for life and enjoy the fruits of many powerful and interesting planetary positions at this point in time. You have what it takes to satisfy your curiosity regarding a burning issue around now, particularly if you are willing to do some investigating when it matters the most.

9 SATURDAY
Moon Age Day 23   Moon Sign Pisces

This would be a rather good time for a charm offensive and for making others take notice of you. The weekend allows you to move closer to achieving one or two longed-for objectives, and you can certainly make sure you are at the forefront of anything that is happening around you in a family sense.

10 SUNDAY
Moon Age Day 24   Moon Sign Aries

Along comes a period during which you need to be emphasising the practical aspects of life, even if some of the people around you are less than helpful. You know what you want and how to get it. The only potential difficulty lies in persuading these reluctant types that the time has come to make changes.

11 MONDAY
Moon Age Day 25   Moon Sign Aries

This is not likely to be one of your luckiest days, at least not by the time the afternoon comes along. The Moon moves into Taurus later on in the day and the lunar low follows. If you are wise you will allow others to take the strain, whilst you sit back and watch any fireworks that ensue.

12 TUESDAY
Moon Age Day 26   Moon Sign Taurus

A low-key phase is now possible, though that does not mean you need to lose out in any way. The only reason for difficulties would be if you tried to make headway against a very strong opposite tide. In other words, if you don't do anything really important, you can ensure that all is well.

13 WEDNESDAY
Moon Age Day 27   Moon Sign Taurus

There can be minor frustrations around but the general picture should be looking stronger by the end of the day. You still should not make major decisions or try to achieve more than would be reasonable during the lunar low but you do have good ideas that can be put into practice later.

14 THURSDAY
Moon Age Day 28   Moon Sign Gemini

Professionally speaking you are now in a better position to make the running. Your powers of persuasion are favoured, and your intuition is deep and penetrating. You know instinctively how to behave and you also now have a better ability to persuade those around you that you know what you are talking about.

15 FRIDAY
Moon Age Day 0   Moon Sign Gemini

The Sun remains in your solar eighth house, a planetary position that is inclined to rake up aspects of the past in such a way as to make you rather nostalgic. This is something that happens to all Water-sign individuals from time to time, and even if it is of no real use, neither should it cause you many problems.

16 SATURDAY
Moon Age Day 1   Moon Sign Cancer

Though your strength lies in asserting yourself as much as possible today, you could find yourself right in the middle of a seesaw. If you push others too hard, they might start to rebel, whereas if you leave them alone altogether, something doesn't get done. Only diplomacy and experience can be your guide under current trends.

17 SUNDAY
Moon Age Day 2   Moon Sign Cancer

You should be well able to express yourself today and at the same time to show a great thirst for change and adventure. What a great time this would be to take a trip – and one that is for personal rather than practical reasons. A good dose of the countryside could do you no end of good.

18 MONDAY
Moon Age Day 3   Moon Sign Leo

If a personal and intimate matter is on your mind at the start of this new week, your best approach is to find someone you can use as a sounding board. You can persuade many people to be your friends at the moment but you will know instinctively which of them you are able to trust deeply.

19 TUESDAY
Moon Age Day 4   Moon Sign Leo

The need to be busy and productive is paramount now, so much so that you might forget that there is a social side to your life too. There should be plenty of scope for mixing business with pleasure and you can make significant contacts that could prove to be extremely useful further down the line.

20 WEDNESDAY *Moon Age Day 5   Moon Sign Leo*

You now have the ability to see others for what they are and to split the people you come across into two definite groups. There are those for whom you care deeply and who you know have your best interests at heart, and then there are individuals who could never be anything more than acquaintances.

21 THURSDAY *Moon Age Day 6   Moon Sign Virgo*

The lengthy transit of Venus through your solar tenth house has favoured relationships for some weeks now, and has helped you to be more sensitive to the feelings of those you care for than might sometimes be the case. Right now it urges you to find the right words of affection and to speak them to an intimate contact.

22 FRIDAY *Moon Age Day 7   Moon Sign Virgo*

Today responds best if you can get beyond your everyday world and experience life as it is lived in slightly different ways. Listening to the experiences of someone who is very different to you could be a start, though you may decide you will have to wear someone else's shoes in order to really move forward.

23 SATURDAY *Moon Age Day 8   Moon Sign Libra*

The signs are that you show yourself to be very practically minded at the moment and will want to have everything just so. This is particularly true at home, where relatives may struggle to keep up with your exacting demands. Don't fall out with anyone simply because they fail to understand what you are trying to say or do.

24 SUNDAY *Moon Age Day 9   Moon Sign Libra*

You would be wise to hang back and use a little caution today, especially when it comes to making money – or at least trying to do so. Things should look markedly better in a day or two but for the moment it's worth holding onto your cash. The Moon is now in your solar twelfth house, heralding a potentially quiet period.

25 MONDAY   *Moon Age Day 10   Moon Sign Libra*

Stand by for action, but not really until tomorrow. If you have the chance to put one or two of your ideas out to tender, then so much the better. This is a day during which you have scope to sharpen your intellect and get ready for a better time to come. Routines can be comforting but might also seem like a chore.

26 TUESDAY   *Moon Age Day 11   Moon Sign Scorpio*

You have great magnetism at your disposal now and can use it to draw people into your ideas. Don't expect to do everything you would wish, because although the lunar high is around you may be setting yourself a very hectic pace. Leave time late in the day for socialising, which probably appeals to you at the moment.

27 WEDNESDAY   *Moon Age Day 12   Moon Sign Scorpio*

You power to have a great effect on life is much increased and you should feel that most of your efforts are bearing fruit. You can afford to spend some time with your lover and also with family members and use some of that dynamism to help them out. Getting what you want in a general sense could be quite easy.

28 THURSDAY   *Moon Age Day 13   Moon Sign Sagittarius*

It's possible that someone today could challenge your perceptions, and if this turns out to be the case you need not be fazed by their presence. On the contrary, they could help you to look at life from a much altered perspective and you can expect to make gains as a result. It won't take you long to build new personal resources at this time.

29 FRIDAY   *Moon Age Day 14   Moon Sign Sagittarius*

Financial matters could well receive a boost at any time now. The Moon is in your solar second house and this allows you to look at old monetary problems from an entirely new perspective. You may be inclined to dwell on the past in personal matters, which probably isn't of much use at the moment.

30 SATURDAY   *Moon Age Day 15*   *Moon Sign Capricorn*

Handling several different tasks at the same time is within your capabilities now. You can relate particularly well to others on an intellectual level, but from an emotional point of view you may do rather less well. The attitude of a particular friend can cause you some concern, though probably with no real justification.

July

2007

1 SUNDAY
☿ *Moon Age Day 16   Moon Sign Capricorn*

You tend to be extremely curious about everything around you now. As a direct contrast to yesterday you should find it easy to work out what makes people tick, and shouldn't be treading on anyone's toes. Most important of all is your diplomacy. It isn't usually your strong point, but you can make sure it is now.

2 MONDAY
☿ *Moon Age Day 17   Moon Sign Capricorn*

This is another good time for taking on ambitious matters. Venus is well placed for you and allows you to look ahead, especially in terms of relationships. If you have been seeking to sweep a particular person off their feet, you could hardly choose a better time than this to do so.

3 TUESDAY
☿ *Moon Age Day 18   Moon Sign Aquarius*

Your domestic life receives a number of important highlights at this time, and this may prompt you to think about certain changes you want to make in and around your home. All family-based matters are well accented, and younger family members especially may give you good cause to be proud of them.

4 WEDNESDAY
☿ *Moon Age Day 19   Moon Sign Aquarius*

If those around you don't appreciate the finer points of your nature, you may have to work especially hard in order to get your message across at the moment. Now is the time to avoid unnecessary routines and push towards new objectives whenever possible. The only drawback if you don't is that life may seem boring.

5 THURSDAY ☿ *Moon Age Day 20   Moon Sign Pisces*

Now you have the ability to display greater openness and should be willing to spill the beans regarding any issue that you have been keeping secret for a while. This tendency to play your cards close to your chest is typical of Scorpio, but is often unnecessary and gets in the way.

6 FRIDAY ☿ *Moon Age Day 21   Moon Sign Pisces*

It's possible that you may decide to play the role of prima donna in certain situations and could be so cranky that it is difficult for others to know how to approach you. Only you can remedy this situation by being as open as possible and by showing how willing you are to co-operate, and most important of all how much you listen.

7 SATURDAY ☿ *Moon Age Day 22   Moon Sign Aries*

Mars in your solar ninth house offers you plenty to look forward to and gives you a chance to increase your energy level. Others might have to virtually run in order to keep up with you, and you can show a great sense of purpose in almost everything. You can make the weekend fast and furious but also extremely interesting.

8 SUNDAY ☿ *Moon Age Day 23   Moon Sign Aries*

There could be some disagreements around today, but you can ensure these are not coming from your direction. If you need to treat certain people with kid gloves, that can be rather wearing. Better by far to stick to those individuals who rarely give you any trouble and who clearly like you.

9 MONDAY ☿ *Moon Age Day 24   Moon Sign Taurus*

The outcome of major decisions may be in some doubt today, which is why you might be best off avoiding them altogether whilst the Moon is in Taurus. Even if you can't make too much progress at the moment, you can still have fun. It's worth opting to do things that are of no special importance.

10 TUESDAY   ☿   *Moon Age Day 25*   *Moon Sign Taurus*

Energy remains in fairly low supply and today responds best if you relax. You can't always be on the move or making decisions, so instead, you may decide to allow others to make the running whilst you stand on the riverbank of life and watch. By tomorrow you can get right back on form and be anxious to move again.

11 WEDNESDAY   *Moon Age Day 26*   *Moon Sign Gemini*

You tend to be able to look at life in a very discriminating way today and may be making subtle changes that can have a great bearing on your life across the days and weeks ahead. Alterations can be subtle but wide-ranging, and friends in particular seem to have what it takes to please you greatly under current influences.

12 THURSDAY   *Moon Age Day 27*   *Moon Sign Gemini*

Trends suggest that you may now feel restless and that you are not making the progress in a material or practical sense that you would wish. Maybe you are looking in the wrong direction or expecting life to work out for you without the necessary effort on your part? More application may be required.

13 FRIDAY   *Moon Age Day 28*   *Moon Sign Cancer*

As a direct contrast to yesterday, your strength lies in your optimism and even excitement. The Sun really starts to shine out in your solar ninth house, offering surprises galore, a wealth of new potentials and a new view of what is necessary to get on better with specific people.

14 SATURDAY   *Moon Age Day 29*   *Moon Sign Cancer*

Be prepared to enjoy what the wider world has to offer this weekend, and you probably won't find this to be the sort of day when you would wish to be stuck at home. The longer the journeys you are able to make, the greater the delights you can find. Long-distance travel could bring especially surprising rewards.

15 SUNDAY
Moon Age Day 0   Moon Sign Cancer

The time is right to look far ahead, and although there is still much to captivate your imagination it is the long-term future that really holds you. Family matters are highlighted, and you could discover a way to help anyone who has been having a difficult time recently.

16 MONDAY
Moon Age Day 1   Moon Sign Leo

Planetary trends now emphasise beneficial social encounters, especially group-related activities. The bigger the group, the better you should feel, and there isn't likely to be a trace of the shyness that Scorpios sometimes exhibit. With everything to play for at work, this is a time of potential advancement.

17 TUESDAY
Moon Age Day 2   Moon Sign Leo

Social trends are definitely on the up and you might even find encounters with those who haven't especially interested you in the past to be filled with possibility today. Don't be surprised if someone is looking at you in a very different light, and might be asking you to take on a particular new task that could be intriguing.

18 WEDNESDAY
Moon Age Day 3   Moon Sign Virgo

Communication is well starred, and there are strong cultural interests to be considered under present planetary trends. If you are not committed to work today you may decide to stimulate the more intellectual qualities within your nature. However, you won't do this by sitting around, so get cracking, Scorpio!

19 THURSDAY
Moon Age Day 4   Moon Sign Virgo

The potential for conflict is quite strong at the moment so it would be just as well for you to avoid confrontational situations if you can. The problem is that if Scorpio feels itself to be cornered, it fights like fury. Before you really get into gear, why not ask yourself whether what you are arguing about is of any consequence?

20 FRIDAY   *Moon Age Day 5   Moon Sign Libra*

This is not really the best time of the month to be stuck with jobs you hate. A better option would be to turn your attention towards more interesting matters. The potential for boredom has rarely been more evident, but you can alleviate the worst potentials by relying on friends who have interesting ideas.

21 SATURDAY   *Moon Age Day 6   Moon Sign Libra*

Today and tomorrow mark a period during which you may well decide to retreat from situations that look taxing. Today offers you a chance to be much more committed to family members than has been the case at any stage so far this month. Home-based routines could seem welcoming.

22 SUNDAY   *Moon Age Day 7   Moon Sign Libra*

Another less than busy day is possible and a time during which you have scope to get to know certain people better. There is probably nothing quiet about you and you should revel in the chance to have a good old chat with just about anyone. The time is right to sit back for a while and enjoy the full benefits of the summer.

23 MONDAY   *Moon Age Day 8   Moon Sign Scorpio*

The lunar high comes along at the start of what has potential to be a busy and eventful sort of week. You have an excellent ability to positively direct your energy and can use this skill to change things you don't care for the look of. If you can get Lady Luck on your side, a few calculated gambles could be in order.

24 TUESDAY   *Moon Age Day 9   Moon Sign Scorpio*

Be prepared to keep up that high profile and use today in order to further your intentions in a professional sense. You have what it takes to get people to listen to you, and their assistance can make all the difference when it matters the most. The odd personal hiccup from earlier days can now be dispelled altogether.

25 WEDNESDAY *Moon Age Day 10 Moon Sign Sagittarius*

Financial security is highlighted, encouraging you to do everything you can to solidify your cash reserves and even to add to them. If there is a major purchase to be made today you need to be very discriminating, because there are potential bargains to be had for Scorpios who shop around.

26 THURSDAY *Moon Age Day 11 Moon Sign Sagittarius*

Your ambition and go-ahead spirit are very well marked under present planetary trends, and although you may still fight like a tiger if you are threatened in any way, in the main you should be able to remain placid and calm. You would be wise to avoid getting tied down with pointless details at any stage during today.

27 FRIDAY *Moon Age Day 12 Moon Sign Sagittarius*

You still have the ability to communicate well, particularly in the direction of friends. It could be that someone you see rarely is around at the moment, and at the same time you may be passing messages back and forth across great distances – maybe the whole world!

28 SATURDAY *Moon Age Day 13 Moon Sign Capricorn*

You now have scope to travel and can take the opportunity to explore a world that looks especially exciting and filled with potential. Scorpio people who chose this period for annual holidays are the luckiest of all, but even a short trip into town or to the country should suit you down to the ground.

29 SUNDAY *Moon Age Day 14 Moon Sign Capricorn*

Trends assist you to get along well with almost everyone, even people who have given you a real problem in the past. You can pesuade even awkward family members to calm down and listen to your timely advice. Your strength lies in making worries disappear like the morning mist under present trends.

30 MONDAY   *Moon Age Day 15   Moon Sign Aquarius*

At the start of a new week you need to widen your intellectual horizons as much as possible, so you shouldn't necessarily stick to things you understand and trust. Taking a chance is part of what life is really about, and you can make great gains if you are willing to push your luck.

31 TUESDAY   *Moon Age Day 16   Moon Sign Aquarius*

The Moon moves into your solar fourth house today and encourages you to turn your attention in the direction of loved ones and towards your home. Even if you feel just a little less sure regarding your own potential, you still have what it takes to get ahead – although the pace may be somewhat slower.

August

2007

1 WEDNESDAY
Moon Age Day 17   Moon Sign Pisces

A new month comes along, offering you scope to seek out hopeful news from those around you. Events generally should put you into a happy frame of mind and new attachments made at this time can prove to be quite fortuitous. Beware of being too quick to apportion blame if things go wrong at work.

2 THURSDAY
Moon Age Day 18   Moon Sign Pisces

Today can be turned into a very fortunate time as far as work is concerned. The Sun remains in your solar tenth house and this helps you to enhance your charm no end. No matter who crosses your path today, you should have something good to say to them. If you make sure people don't forget this, in the end this stands you in good stead.

3 FRIDAY
Moon Age Day 19   Moon Sign Aries

It's worth making sure that you are slightly more organised than seems to have been the case earlier in the week. Romance is positively highlighted under present trends, and if you have been keeping your eye open for a possible new attachment, this might be as good a time as any to focus your attention.

4 SATURDAY
Moon Age Day 20   Moon Sign Aries

There is a strong social dimension to this weekend, and Saturday is the best day of all for making merry in some way. It could be that new influences entering your life around now offer you a greater sense of purpose to your activities, but at the same time you have what it takes to make life entertaining for everyone.

5 SUNDAY
Moon Age Day 21   Moon Sign Taurus

If things slow down somewhat, there may not be much you can do about the situation but to relax and let life pass you by for a few hours. You won't miss much, and in any case it is vitally important to recharge your batteries whilst the lunar low is around. A day to avoid getting embroiled in what seems like a family soap opera.

6 MONDAY
Moon Age Day 22   Moon Sign Taurus

You may well have less time to spend on personal goals today because there are all sorts of little issues that need resolving. This might not be easy whilst the Moon is in Taurus but if you are wise you will seek some assistance. You can get almost anyone to help you out if you are not too proud to ask.

7 TUESDAY
Moon Age Day 23   Moon Sign Taurus

Professional matters seem to get something of a lift today, even though you may still not be feeling on top form. If the attitude of friends and family members is decidedly odd, extra patience will be necessary. Keep a sense of proportion when it comes to spending money, or better still, save it for now.

8 WEDNESDAY
Moon Age Day 24   Moon Sign Gemini

The need to simplify your life is heightened under present trends and the last thing you need is any sort of complication. This is especially true in terms of personal attachments, and you would be wise to keep things as settled and steady as you can. A favourable time to find ways to enjoy the summer weather.

9 THURSDAY
Moon Age Day 25   Moon Sign Gemini

What a good day this would be for making career decisions or for moving forward into new pastures. Acting on impulse should come more naturally now and there seem to be less complications in your life. Routines are acceptable, but there may still be moments when you will want to break out into new territory.

10 FRIDAY
Moon Age Day 26   Moon Sign Cancer

Don't be afraid to open up to loved ones and listen carefully to what they are telling you. Even if you find some difficulty at first with regard to a new interest or pastime, in the main you need the stimulus that comes from looking at situations in a different way. Friends may well be encouraging you to take a chance.

11 SATURDAY
Moon Age Day 27   Moon Sign Cancer

This would be another good day for concentrating on professional issues, even though the weekend might not seem to be the best time for such matters. Rather than actually achieving much, you have scope to look ahead and plan carefully. By all means give yourself a pat on the back for a domestic issue that is now resolved.

12 SUNDAY
Moon Age Day 28   Moon Sign Leo

Venus is now in your solar tenth house and this supports your efforts to make greater progress, especially in matters associated with love. Although there is still a long way to go with regard to some matters, you are able to move forward steadily towards your planned objectives.

13 MONDAY
Moon Age Day 0   Moon Sign Leo

Emotional or domestic pressures could be increased by the presence of Mars in your solar eighth house. It certainly means new starts of one sort or another, possibly as a result of arguments. Be extra careful today because you may be more than usually susceptible to minor mishaps.

14 TUESDAY
Moon Age Day 1   Moon Sign Virgo

Your talent for dealing with slightly awkward people is highlighted today and you needn't surrender your patience just because things sometimes go wrong. All of this helps you to mark yourself out as special. This is particularly true in terms of the way someone sees you as a potential romantic mate.

15 WEDNESDAY
Moon Age Day 2   Moon Sign Virgo

Be prepared to get yourself involved with groups of people today, either inside or outside of work. You co-operate well and have what it takes to be a natural leader in most situations. Even on those occasions when you lack personal confidence, you can make sure this doesn't show to others.

16 THURSDAY
Moon Age Day 3   Moon Sign Virgo

This could be a day of deep insights and a time when you have scope to show the strong intuitive qualities of Scorpio. For this reason you should move forward by listening to your inner mind. Normal common sense is fine, but is probably not so useful to you when it comes to personal relationships today.

17 FRIDAY
Moon Age Day 4   Moon Sign Libra

You have the opportunity to bring some discipline and determination to the way you are moving forward in your career. Scorpio people who are presently in full-time education will of course be on holiday now, but today is a chance to look at certain projects ahead of a new start in September.

18 SATURDAY
Moon Age Day 5   Moon Sign Libra

Those of you who work at the weekend could turn out to be the luckiest of all today. There is a strong chance that you can win the good advice and the deep confidence of either a superior or a more experienced colleague. If on the other hand your time is your own, it's worth opting for something different and exciting if you can.

19 SUNDAY
Moon Age Day 6   Moon Sign Scorpio

Your sense of purpose has rarely been better, and with everything to play for in the romantic stakes you can make this a Sunday to remember. The time is right to sweep your partner off their feet by planning something on the spur of the moment, and don't be frightened to spend just a little money whilst the lunar high is around.

20 MONDAY   *Moon Age Day 7   Moon Sign Scorpio*

You can afford to express confidence and faith in your own abilities whilst the Moon remains in your zodiac sign. Even if others prove to be difficult, you have what it takes to plough on regardless and to be very impressive to those who are around you. You can make this an excellent start to a new working week.

21 TUESDAY   *Moon Age Day 8   Moon Sign Scorpio*

The focus is on making contacts, and your personal magnetism appears to be extremely high. Although you won't break any records today you do have what it takes to stick at tasks until you have completed them to your own satisfaction. Above all you can be very impressive.

22 WEDNESDAY   *Moon Age Day 9   Moon Sign Sagittarius*

The prospects look good for further positive moves in terms of your career. A whole host of planetary influences now gather and conspire to offer you the chance to make some sort of new start. There is a slight tendency for you to act on impulse, but you can afford to trust yourself because it looks as though you know what you are doing.

23 THURSDAY   *Moon Age Day 10   Moon Sign Sagittarius*

The way you deal with any minor challenges to your authority sets you apart as being quite special. Instead of flying off the handle you should be able to remain patient and willing to explain your own point of view. This attitude could well gain you friends and allies when it probably matters a good deal.

24 FRIDAY   *Moon Age Day 11   Moon Sign Capricorn*

Getting your ideas across is just as vital today as actually achieving anything in a concrete sense. This is a time for planning because when you have finished doing so the job itself should prove to be easy. It's worth getting others on board and using your good communication skills to explain any tricky issues.

25 SATURDAY   *Moon Age Day 12   Moon Sign Capricorn*

This can be a period of significant advancement in terms of the way you are able to deal with family matters. You can make sure that anything that has been a real problem to you in the past now finds its own answer. In particular, if there has been some sort of estrangement, life offers ways in which to put things right.

26 SUNDAY   *Moon Age Day 13   Moon Sign Aquarius*

If you feel more sensitive than usual right now, you may decide to look for a little solitude on this high summer Sunday. You could be happiest pulling up a few weeds in the garden or else spending a few hours in the sunshine with a good book. Relatives may now be more difficult to understand.

27 MONDAY   *Moon Age Day 14   Moon Sign Aquarius*

Venus in its present position offers a boost to career-based issues during a month that has been very much geared towards personal advancement. Although you might find that not everyone is thinking about things in quite the way that you are, you do have a good ability to talk anyone round. All it takes is your natural charisma.

28 TUESDAY   *Moon Age Day 15   Moon Sign Aquarius*

If personal ambitions suddenly seem less crucial than they have done in earlier days, you may be happy to settle for a quieter day all round. You have what it takes to attract love from family members and in particular your partner. Don't be afraid to show a return on their investment in you.

29 WEDNESDAY   *Moon Age Day 16   Moon Sign Pisces*

This is a time during which social meetings may have a special significance and a period during which you are once again able to use that famous Scorpio intuition. Even if there is a little more luck about, this is certainly not an ideal time to be thinking about gambling. Rather than spending you should be saving for the moment.

30 THURSDAY *Moon Age Day 17   Moon Sign Pisces*

Benefits can be gained from career matters and from keeping up a generally busy pace. Today would be good for visiting friends if you have time. If there is a new arrival announced somewhere in the family you should offer the necessary congratulations and these will be very welcome.

31 FRIDAY *Moon Age Day 18   Moon Sign Aries*

The last day of August could well find you somewhat sluggish in your thinking and your actions. You need to think very careful about subsequent moves, and would be wise not to rush your fences. As a result of all this you may find today rather tedious when compared with others earlier in the month, though it offers a useful interlude.

September

2007

1 SATURDAY
Moon Age Day 19   Moon Sign Aries

Everyday life could be subject to certain defeats and delays, though most of these come later in the day, as the Moon moves slowly into Taurus. Although you may not be expecting too much of yourself or others, it's worth remaining optimistic because any difficulties are temporary. Awkward matters might need to be shelved for a few days.

2 SUNDAY
Moon Age Day 20   Moon Sign Taurus

Some irritating elements could well accompany any efforts to get ahead right now and the best way to deal with life is to sit back and relax. This may not be easy, particularly if you feel things will collapse without your individual effort. Now is the time to have faith in yourself and in your life.

3 MONDAY
Moon Age Day 21   Moon Sign Taurus

This is a good time for forging the right type of social contacts and for making the most of what life is offering you free of charge. There are new incentives to be considered this week and you might find this to be an excellent time to take a holiday. Even if you are stuck at home, you can still have fun.

4 TUESDAY
Moon Age Day 22   Moon Sign Gemini

Scorpios who have been looking for a new job should really keep their eyes open today. The greatest progress you can make at the moment is in the professional sphere of your life. Even if things are a little slow at the start of the day, you can make things happen by simply being in the right place at the right time.

5 WEDNESDAY *Moon Age Day 23   Moon Sign Gemini*

Expanding your horizons is what today is about, and you should take to new opportunities like a duck to water. This has potential to be an excellent week, and you can be especially good when it comes to getting your notions across to others. Don't be surprised if new personalities enter your life at any time now.

6 THURSDAY *Moon Age Day 24   Moon Sign Cancer*

You have considerable personal charm available, and can use it to get more of what you want from life. Intuitive and understanding, you should do all you can to make the lot of others easier. This is especially true of loved ones, but you needn't restrict yourself to those you know.

7 FRIDAY *Moon Age Day 25   Moon Sign Cancer*

You may find yourself slightly at odds with someone today, and if so it is important that you keep your temper. Even if others are losing their cool, by keeping yours you stand the best chance of winning out in the end. The attitude of a colleague could be difficult to understand, but give it time and things should become clear.

8 SATURDAY *Moon Age Day 26   Moon Sign Leo*

You now have scope to use original and quite unique ways of making more ground in a financial sense. A particularly good idea should be pursued, because you could have just come up with a real winner. One option is to seek out people who are in the know, explain your notion to them and see how they can help you.

9 SUNDAY *Moon Age Day 27   Moon Sign Leo*

Trends encourage you to identify with the aims of the group, so your usual staunch individuality may be of less use to you right now. It is easy for Scorpio to go with the flow, and you should be able to persuade others within the group that you should be in charge of things. A good social day is indicated.

10 MONDAY
Moon Age Day 28   Moon Sign Leo

You function best today when you can mix your own skills with those of others. As a result, group activities are still well highlighted. You have what it takes to heal a breach that might have formed a long time ago, and your ability to bring together those who have been estranged for ages is significant at present.

11 TUESDAY
Moon Age Day 29   Moon Sign Virgo

There are signs that your ideas are very much influenced now by what others think. Of course it's good to bear other points of view in mind, but you might get on slightly better if you stick to your own guns. The only real problem lies in having to do things that you know in your heart are bound to be a waste of time.

12 WEDNESDAY
Moon Age Day 0   Moon Sign Virgo

You may not feel quite as confident today as you have been doing so far this month. The Moon is not in an especially good position for you, and it may be harder to persuade others to lend their support. Do keep an open mind about social possibilities, because a change of some sort would do you good.

13 THURSDAY
Moon Age Day 1   Moon Sign Libra

Accomplishments are made today through sheer determination and strength of will. Scorpio possesses the ability to keep going when others have fallen by the wayside, and this is particularly emphasised under present trends. Even jobs that look more or less impossible shouldn't be beyond you.

14 FRIDAY
Moon Age Day 2   Moon Sign Libra

Today offers you scope to thrive in situations that mean you have to meet new people, which is not always the case for Scorpio. The more interesting these individuals may be, the greater is the incentive you can get from them. Social stimulation is also the key to success whilst present planetary trends prevail.

15 SATURDAY   *Moon Age Day 3   Moon Sign Scorpio*

The lunar high merely adds to a fairly fortunate planetary line-up that exists for you at present. In particular it strengthens your eighth-house Mars, which assists you to move closer to achieving longed-for objectives. You don't suffer fools gladly, and may decide to push on alone if you have to.

16 SUNDAY   *Moon Age Day 4   Moon Sign Scorpio*

A strong feeling of affluence is a legacy of present trends. Even if you decide to spend more lavishly, financial trends fortunately look stronger in order to compensate. Your charm isn't in doubt and you have what it takes to get on extremely well with the most exciting and dynamic people you know.

17 MONDAY   *Moon Age Day 5   Moon Sign Scorpio*

This is a time during which you need to focus on your aims and aspirations. Life may not exactly be giving you anything on a plate, but you don't care about that because you are now so able to take what you want. You can remain kind and supportive, but maybe slightly more inclined to feather your own nest.

18 TUESDAY   *Moon Age Day 6   Moon Sign Sagittarius*

Once again involvements with groups are well favoured and will continue to be so as long as the Sun remains in your solar eleventh house. Make the most of opportunities to encounter the new and unusual in life right now, as this offers a greater sense of fascination. The strange things others do may be of particular interest.

19 WEDNESDAY   *Moon Age Day 7   Moon Sign Sagittarius*

Mercury is now in your solar twelfth house and this planetary position can have certain drawbacks. Overlooking life's practical details is one of them, so it is very important to pay attention in everything you are doing. A bloomer made now might take days to put right!

20 THURSDAY   *Moon Age Day 8   Moon Sign Capricorn*

The signs are that you are very much on the move today and anxious not to allow either yourself or life to stand still. If there is any frustration here it comes from the fact that you cannot get others to adopt quite the pace that seems natural to you. Your best approach would be simply to do a few things on your own.

21 FRIDAY   *Moon Age Day 9   Moon Sign Capricorn*

Circumstances may press in on you, and you might not be offering the best of what you can be to the world at large. A slight feeling of lethargy is possible, as is some annoyance if things don't go your way. Patience can work wonders, but so can a little time spent on your own so that you can meditate.

22 SATURDAY   *Moon Age Day 10   Moon Sign Capricorn*

You may decide that your home offers a refuge from pressures that may be building up in the outside world. There are times when it is useful for Scorpio to stand still and take stock. You are entering one of these periods, and it will do you no harm at all to take a few hours to be with those you love.

23 SUNDAY   *Moon Age Day 11   Moon Sign Aquarius*

The Sun has now entered your solar twelfth house, and although this is by no means bad news for you it can frustrate some of your intentions. You may have to work that much harder in order to get what you want most during the next few weeks, but Scorpio knows all about hard work.

24 MONDAY   *Moon Age Day 12   Moon Sign Aquarius*

Trends encourage you to be more of a private person than has been the case during most of September. When you are in this frame of mind it is difficult for anyone to get through to you, which is partly why you may decide to spend at least some time completely on your own. This is a phase that should soon pass.

25 TUESDAY   *Moon Age Day 13   Moon Sign Pisces*

In a direct contrast to yesterday, today's planetary trends are especially good for social mixing and for being in happy company. You can afford to get involved in new interests and should relish the chance to make yourself the centre of attention. Romance is especially well highlighted at this stage of the week.

26 WEDNESDAY   *Moon Age Day 14   Moon Sign Pisces*

This is not exactly the best time for putting your personal skills to the test. On the contrary, you might be much better off allowing others to make some of the decisions, whilst you stand back and watch. Today responds best if you keep your ambitions within bounds and leave all new starts for a day or two.

27 THURSDAY   *Moon Age Day 15   Moon Sign Aries*

Even if you prove yourself to be an efficient worker today, you still may not have what it takes to risk everything on individual decisions. Rules and regulations may get on your nerves, and seeking an uncomplicated life as much as possible would be no bad thing. Today could be good for shopping.

28 FRIDAY   *Moon Age Day 16   Moon Sign Aries*

What goes on in your professional environment could help you to put a real smile on your face and you can make progress even when you think it isn't possible to do so. In a personal sense you need to be careful not to give in to morbid fears that are based solely on the way your mind is working and not in reality.

29 SATURDAY   *Moon Age Day 17   Moon Sign Taurus*

The lunar low arrives and it will hardly do anything to make you more optimistic. If you bear in mind that this is a very temporary matter, you should be able to avoid getting down in the dumps. Why not seek support from friends, who might also offer some incentives that will lift the weekend for you?

30 SUNDAY

Moon Age Day 18   Moon Sign Taurus

You can easily stumble over obstacles, but if you refuse to get involved in awkward matters you will be better off. There is a tendency for you to seek ego gratification today and to expect others to be complimenting you all the time. This is probably born of insecurity, and is fortunately a temporary thing.

October
2007

1 MONDAY
Moon Age Day 19   Moon Sign Gemini

Today offers you scope to experience life at an emotional level. Intuition is strong and can guide you accurately when it comes to making the right decisions, though you may not be as practical as would often be the case. As the day wears on your more vocal side is to the fore, especially when you're with friends.

2 TUESDAY
Moon Age Day 20   Moon Sign Gemini

Your selfless attitude has a strong part to play in relationships at this time. Be prepared to show your willingness to do almost anything for others, especially in terms of family relationships. If you are not getting on at work quite as well as you would wish, your best response is to show a little patience.

3 WEDNESDAY
Moon Age Day 21   Moon Sign Cancer

It's possible that what once seemed like a sound and practical idea is now less appealing, and you could find that you are working very hard to no real end. One fact about Scorpio that is always present is your resistance to giving in, and though this is usually a laudable quality, it might mean even more toil for nothing now.

4 THURSDAY
Moon Age Day 22   Moon Sign Cancer

This would be an excellent time to travel for fun. Even if what you are doing is entirely practical in nature, you can enjoy yourself on the way. There has rarely been a better time for Scorpio to mix business with pleasure, and you can seek out chances to revel in the company of the sort of people who have a delightful madness about them.

5 FRIDAY
Moon Age Day 23   Moon Sign Leo

Information you can get from colleagues and friends now might help you to throw some light on a mystery from the past. Try to reach out to people in different walks of life and learn from what they have to say. You are gradually climbing into a much stronger personal position and should be getting back some of that earlier optimism.

6 SATURDAY
Moon Age Day 24   Moon Sign Leo

Finances and material concerns are not highlighted to the same extent as they were a few days ago. The weekend is more about enjoying yourself rather than increasing your income. Your greatest source of reward comes from being able to get yourself in the right sort of company and from opening up more.

7 SUNDAY
Moon Age Day 25   Moon Sign Leo

This would be a good day to do something recreational. At the same time you can be quite creative and can use this trait to produce results from all your efforts. On a slightly negative slant you need to be careful about what you say in open discussions. It is quite possible to give offence without intending to do so.

8 MONDAY
Moon Age Day 26   Moon Sign Virgo

You can now capitalise on a phase of busy action. Mercury has entered your solar first house and this enables you to pep up your life no end. Communications generally are well starred, and there is a certain sense of excitement that is going to be around for a week or two at least. You certainly should not get bored.

9 TUESDAY
Moon Age Day 27   Moon Sign Virgo

If you need some help today, it shouldn't be very far away. You should also find moments for quiet reflection, which is necessary if the actions you are going to take are well thought out. It's worth allowing family members a little more leeway than might have been the case recently.

10 WEDNESDAY   *Moon Age Day 28   Moon Sign Libra*

As the Moon is now in your solar twelfth house, you could be a bit more socially reluctant than usual. Trends encourage an urge to spend moments on your own, and you may decide not to get involved in anything new for the next couple of days. None of this should prevent you from being well organised or professionally active.

11 THURSDAY   *Moon Age Day 0   Moon Sign Libra*

You natural sense of compassion now assists you to help those who are less well off than you are. This is also a good time to be with friends, but not a particularly useful period for inviting strangers into your life. You may still not be firing on all cylinders in a strictly social sense.

12 FRIDAY   ☿   *Moon Age Day 1   Moon Sign Libra*

With a slow start to the day you might be very surprised at the way things speed up later on. Your best approach under current influences is to avoid pointless routines and spend as much time as you can thinking about the new possibilities that stand all around you. By tomorrow you should be in a position to get stuck in big time.

13 SATURDAY   ☿   *Moon Age Day 2   Moon Sign Scorpio*

The Moon now moves into Scorpio. This fact, taken together with that first-house Mercury, helps you to make this the most dynamic day of the month. If you can get Lady Luck on your side, you can afford to take more risks in the knowledge that your capacity for looking and thinking ahead is extremely good.

14 SUNDAY   ☿   *Moon Age Day 3   Moon Sign Scorpio*

If you have a pet project, now is the best time of all to work on it. You can persuade almost everyone to lend a hand and if there is any problem at all about today it lies in the fact that your very popularity makes it difficult to concentrate. You would be wise to stay away from arguments that have nothing to do with you.

15 MONDAY ☿ *Moon Age Day 4* *Moon Sign Sagittarius*

Money-making concerns are highlighted, and you can use your knack of hanging on to cash you already possess. Don't be surprised if you discover that you have an admirer you didn't suspect previously. In every sense you can make sure your popularity is going off the scale.

16 TUESDAY ☿ *Moon Age Day 5* *Moon Sign Sagittarius*

Communication is positively highlighted under present trends, and you are also in a good position to see all sides of specific issues. In a work sense you should not provide opponents with the very ammunition they need by admitted your shortcomings. The truth is important, but only up to a point today.

17 WEDNESDAY ☿ *Moon Age Day 6* *Moon Sign Sagittarius*

You may meet someone today who challenges your views or who really makes you work hard to explain yourself. This is not necessarily a bad thing, especially if it shakes you out of some sort of lethargy that has overtaken you. You needn't let anything threaten your overall success.

18 THURSDAY ☿ *Moon Age Day 7* *Moon Sign Capricorn*

There are signs that you may spend a lot of time at the moment trying to work out what loved ones are thinking. This is not a wasted exercise because as a result of your efforts you might be able to make someone else much happier. Your concern for those you love is always on display, even when you are busy with other things.

19 FRIDAY ☿ *Moon Age Day 8* *Moon Sign Capricorn*

Your desire for knowledge is to the fore, encouraging you to spend a lot of time today casting around to make yourself even more knowledgeable. Not only do you want to know things but you also want to communicate what you have learned to others. There are gains to be made financially, but not by gambling.

20 SATURDAY   ☿ *Moon Age Day 9   Moon Sign Aquarius*

This is a day to gain some domestic tranquillity and a period during which you may be happy to spend time in the bosom of your family. You can push yourself to other things if you really try, though it could seem that small blockages are placed upon your actions. Don't worry, because this is an entirely temporary phenomenon.

21 SUNDAY   ☿ *Moon Age Day 10   Moon Sign Aquarius*

If ever there was a good time to start new projects, that is what this Sunday represents. You should have the time to think things through and to plan, but not for long if you have a burning desire to get on and achieve something. Neither need your efforts be restricted to domestic or home-based issues.

22 MONDAY   ☿ *Moon Age Day 11   Moon Sign Pisces*

You have scope to become the centre of attention as a new working week gets started, and the social aspects of life could now seem just as important as the practical or professional ones. Stand by to go out and discover love, especially if you are presently without a permanent romantic attachment.

23 TUESDAY   ☿ *Moon Age Day 12   Moon Sign Pisces*

Your present fondness for debate may now be put to the test, and winning may take some hard work. Not that this fact should trouble you because this is a period during which you are encouraged to sharpen your intellect and to get to grips with issues that have been murky in the past.

24 WEDNESDAY ☿ *Moon Age Day 13   Moon Sign Pisces*

At last the Sun enters your solar first house and the time for personal rejuvenation is at hand. Even if there have been significant obstacles around with the Sun in your twelfth house, you can put all of that out of the way now. The time is right to look towards your objectives with renewed enthusiasm and a greater sense of purpose.

25 THURSDAY ☿ *Moon Age Day 14 Moon Sign Aries*

Even if your drive to achieve things is getting stronger all the time, a little caution is advised for the moment. You can be too impetuous for your own good, and might be inclined to fly off the handle if things don't go the way you want them to. Why not exercise a little patience and count to ten before reacting?

26 FRIDAY ☿ *Moon Age Day 15 Moon Sign Aries*

Beware of making any hasty decisions, especially later on today. The lunar low is in the offing and proves to be stronger as it arrives than it will be across the weekend. This may be because Saturday and Sunday bring more personal associations, whereas today could see you in the thick of professional matters.

27 SATURDAY ☿ *Moon Age Day 16 Moon Sign Taurus*

Although this might not be the most exciting or dynamic day of the month, you needn't let the lunar low spoil what can be a very enjoyable weekend. A day to keep your wishes moderate and your actions considered. If you decide to spend time with family members and friends, you can pack much enjoyment into today.

28 SUNDAY ☿ *Moon Age Day 17 Moon Sign Taurus*

Trends encourage you to be preoccupied with the past and inclined to give in to nostalgia. The only piece of advice that counts today is to keep yourself entirely focused on the future and to avoid dwelling on matters that have gone. You can afford to help any friends who need your assistance now.

29 MONDAY ☿ *Moon Age Day 18   Moon Sign Gemini*

Enthusiasm is to the fore and you should be well able to accept the positive trends brought about by the position of the Sun in your solar first house. Most of all you are very creative and can make things happen with just a click of the finger and thumb. Scorpio is a real wizard, and can make everyone take notice.

30 TUESDAY ☿ *Moon Age Day 19   Moon Sign Gemini*

If you don't express yourself quite as clearly today as seems to be necessary, some misunderstandings can crop up. Do your best to explain yourself fully and especially so if you are dealing with ideas that are quite clear to you but fairly obscure to colleagues and superiors.

31 WEDNESDAY ☿ *Moon Age Day 20   Moon Sign Cancer*

Freedom is the key to happiness on the last day of October, and you may not be very pleased if circumstances conspire to hold you back in any way. There is a certain restlessness about you today that can best be dealt with by pushing forward and by refusing to take no for an answer.

November 2007

1 THURSDAY ☿ *Moon Age Day 21   Moon Sign Cancer*

There is a strong desire to lead the field as a new month gets started. If you feel that some of your desires are not being met, now is the time to put in the extra effort necessary to bring them to fruition. All of this might make you rather cranky on occasions, especially if circumstances or people get in your way.

2 FRIDAY ☿ *Moon Age Day 22   Moon Sign Leo*

In a social sense you have what it takes to be charming and friendly – just right to improve your general popularity and to get others to help you out. You should be very much at home when in large groups of people and will be quite happy to communicate your ideas to anyone. In almost every sense you can make this a red-letter day.

3 SATURDAY *Moon Age Day 23   Moon Sign Leo*

When it comes to practical matters you can afford to be at the head of things and to take the lead under almost all opportunities. You should remain independent, confident and sure of your point of view. There might be just a little frustration around if other people get in your way or fail to appreciate your point of view.

4 SUNDAY *Moon Age Day 24   Moon Sign Virgo*

Trends assist you to enjoy the cut and thrust of everyday life and to make this Sunday special with just a little extra effort. Rather than concentrating too much on practical matters, it's worth getting out of bed intending to enjoy what comes your way. If an offer of some sort of outing comes along, be prepared to grab it with both hands!

5 MONDAY
Moon Age Day 25   Moon Sign Virgo

Don't be afraid to lap up attention today and take great delight in being the centre of attention. This is likely to be especially true at work, where your motivational skills are also well starred. In a more personal sense you may fail to persuade your partner that you really do know what you are talking about.

6 TUESDAY
Moon Age Day 26   Moon Sign Libra

There are some small gains to be made at the moment, though this is hardly likely to be a sensational sort of day. It's worth planning now for the end of the week because that is when trends come best for you. You shouldn't have any trouble following complicated instructions if you make sure you have your thinking head on.

7 WEDNESDAY
Moon Age Day 27   Moon Sign Libra

You might quite rightly have doubts about those who are talking big but actually producing very little. Your strength, on the other hand, lies in not making promises you cannot follow up on, and in being extremely reliable. Today offers a chance to get in touch with those you know have the answers you presently need.

8 THURSDAY
Moon Age Day 28   Moon Sign Libra

Your sensitivity may affect a loved one in a subtle and quite unexpected way and it is possible that your intuition is also working very strongly. Time spent on your own today is certainly not wasted, and you may even be able to come up with some of the answers that those around you have searched for diligently.

9 FRIDAY
Moon Age Day 0   Moon Sign Scorpio

The lunar high comes as an empowering influence this time round and allows you to make progress in most spheres of your life. You needn't take no for an answer, and tend to be very single-minded when it matters the most. You can also make the most of the fact that your level of general good luck is excellent.

10 SATURDAY *Moon Age Day 1   Moon Sign Scorpio*

You can get the tide of fortune to flow your way, so much so that you are far more willing to take a chance than will have been the case earlier in the week. They say that fortune favours the bold, and if this is the case you are likely to get on very well today. Be brave enough to tell someone how special they are to you.

11 SUNDAY *Moon Age Day 2   Moon Sign Sagittarius*

The ability to deal with practical matters in the way you did yesterday now seems to be slightly lacking. This may be as much down to the reaction of others as it is to your own nature. If there is something about which you are uncertain, you could do far worse than asking someone more experienced.

12 MONDAY *Moon Age Day 3   Moon Sign Sagittarius*

Confidence should be stronger today, and you really notice the first-house Sun that is so strong in your chart at the moment. Make the most of this powerful interlude by committing yourself to plans that are audacious but certainly not impossible. You can make people marvel at your present ability to get things right first time.

13 TUESDAY *Moon Age Day 4   Moon Sign Sagittarius*

Today you can show yourself to be very resourceful and more than able to get what you want, even from potentially difficult situations. You needn't take no for an answer, and can be more persuasive than even Scorpio usually manages to be. Pointless rules and regulations might simply make you more determined.

14 WEDNESDAY *Moon Age Day 5   Moon Sign Capricorn*

You are very inclined to take up mental pursuits today, whether or not they are of practical use to you. Any intellectual challenge could really capture your attention under present trends, so much so that everything else may be ignored. Once again there are gains to made if you show yourself to be single-minded.

15 THURSDAY   *Moon Age Day 6   Moon Sign Capricorn*

Do others presently have your best interests at heart? It might appear so, but you need to be slightly careful because it is entirely possible that at least one person is trying to deceive you in some way. It would be sensible to check and double-check all details today, and to analyse situations very carefully.

16 FRIDAY   *Moon Age Day 7   Moon Sign Aquarius*

Planetary trends now favour hearth and home, and you may not be quite so showy or up-front as has been the case throughout much of this week. Many Scorpios might decide to put their feet up when the day's work is done, and there is certainly nothing wrong with wanting to take a complete break.

17 SATURDAY   *Moon Age Day 8   Moon Sign Aquarius*

Mars is presently in your solar ninth house, and although its position there can help to quicken your mind and also offers flashes of brilliance, there is a downside. It also enhances your argumentative side, especially when others won't go along with something about which you are more than certain.

18 SUNDAY   *Moon Age Day 9   Moon Sign Aquarius*

You have what it takes to be both magnetic and dynamic today, and as a result you can make sure that others love to be around you. The time is right to put your creative powers to the test and start something new around your home. If your ideas are particularly grandiose, you may decide to enlist the support of other family members.

19 MONDAY   *Moon Age Day 10   Moon Sign Pisces*

You now have the ability to go well beyond the status quo and that means really allowing your originality to shine out. The only slight drawback is that you can be a little shy if you have to stand up in front of a crowd. This should be less of a problem whilst the Sun retains its present position.

20 TUESDAY   *Moon Age Day 11   Moon Sign Pisces*

There are signs that an issue to do with your love life may seem slightly less than inspiring today. Maybe your partner is simply not receptive to your ideas or it could be that they are simply out of sorts with themselves. Whatever the problem, you should be able to find the patience and the sensitivity to deal with it.

21 WEDNESDAY   *Moon Age Day 12   Moon Sign Aries*

Travel and cultural pursuits are at the top of the agenda now, so some of you may be taking a late but welcome break. This would do you a great deal of good and get you into the right frame of mind to face the upcoming lunar low. Your sense of fun is highlighted and you have what it takes to enjoy good company.

22 THURSDAY   *Moon Age Day 13   Moon Sign Aries*

This is not what could be called a good period for taking undue risks. Before the end of the day the Moon will have entered Taurus, its worst position as far as you are concerned. Be prepared to use a little circumspection, and don't be afraid to seek out some inspiration and experience when it matters the most.

23 FRIDAY   *Moon Age Day 14   Moon Sign Taurus*

Your strengths in general are probably not up to par, and you may decide you would rather sit and watch the world go by than be directly involved in almost anything now. That's fine, just as long as you realise that something you have been working hard to achieve needs just a little attention.

24 SATURDAY   *Moon Age Day 15   Moon Sign Taurus*

Monetary security is to the fore today, and you may decide to sit on your purse or wallet rather than hand over cash when you don't have to do so. When dealing with younger family members you show that you are capable of being strict but fair, though you would also be wise to explain yourself.

25 SUNDAY
Moon Age Day 16   Moon Sign Gemini

Trends encourage you to bring your experience into play and show yourself to be particularly attentive to the needs of family members. This is a very mixed sort of day but is a period during which you can finalise details for plans that have a bearing on Christmas. Scorpio should definitely be looking ahead now.

26 MONDAY
Moon Age Day 17   Moon Sign Gemini

Everyday affairs should run smoothly enough, whilst you have scope to show just how funny you can be. Humour is the way to get what you want at the moment and the fact is hardly likely to be lost on you. All cultural interests captivate you now, and you can make sure your intellect is as honed as a razor under nearly all circumstances.

27 TUESDAY
Moon Age Day 18   Moon Sign Cancer

Money and the good things of life generally could be there for the taking, even if you don't recognise the fact at first. Don't be slow when it comes to telling the world what you want, because it's likely that others will be on the same wavelength. You won't achieve anything at all by keeping quiet.

28 WEDNESDAY
Moon Age Day 19   Moon Sign Cancer

You may desire greater freedom, but the big question is how to get it? Instead of showing your independence, why not rely on the good offices and ideas of others? At work you can afford to take on responsibility and be speedy in getting things done. Meanwhile, domestic matters are likely to be put on hold.

29 THURSDAY
Moon Age Day 20   Moon Sign Leo

When in pursuit of personal achievement you need to be quite subtle today. There is no point in trying to bulldoze others into your way of thinking because you might simply cause them to become more entrenched in their own attitudes. It's worth seeking the opinions of others, especially if you know that their point of view is sound.

30 FRIDAY
Moon Age Day 21   Moon Sign Leo

The planetary picture provides excellent opportunities for small financial gains, some of which could come like a bolt from the blue. You have potential to outsmart the competition, both at work and in social activities or sports. With the weekend ahead you have an opportunity to pursue a particular idea for having fun.

December

2007

1 SATURDAY
Moon Age Day 22   Moon Sign Virgo

In a social sense you may well be anxious to get some change working in your life. Influences indicate a very restless time for Scorpio, and you may not always feel entirely comfortable with your lot. There are exciting times ahead and you should instinctively realise that this is the case, even if getting things moving takes a while.

2 SUNDAY
Moon Age Day 23   Moon Sign Virgo

Money-making potential reaches a peak around now, motivating you to be far more committed to gaining cash than you are to spending it. Will this cause issues with family members and especially your partner? Well, that all depends on the way you deal with them. You certainly can't afford to look like a Scrooge!

3 MONDAY
Moon Age Day 24   Moon Sign Virgo

Getting some peace and privacy may not be very easy at the moment, particularly if others are calling on your assistance all the time. If it isn't family members who demand your attention it could be friends. You may simply decide not to react however, because basically you need to be needed.

4 TUESDAY
Moon Age Day 25   Moon Sign Libra

Conflicts can arise if you sense that certain people are showing a lack of sensitivity to your own circumstances. Neither will you stand idly by if you think that a friend is being misused in any way. Scorpio's social conscience is extremely heightened under present trends, so why not use this to help yourself and others?

5 WEDNESDAY
Moon Age Day 26   Moon Sign Libra

You are now in a position to gain greater control of your personal finances, as well as being able to impose a degree of discipline regarding the spending of others. This is some achievement so close to Christmas, but you should capitalise on good ideas for saving money.

6 THURSDAY
Moon Age Day 27   Moon Sign Scorpio

This is a time for grasping nettles firmly, because you have all it takes to be in control of your own destiny. If there is something going on in your life that you don't care for, it's worth sorting it out today and tomorrow. The lunar high enables you to use more luck than usual and even to increase your social standing.

7 FRIDAY
Moon Age Day 28   Moon Sign Scorpio

Trends encourage you to show a great deal of faith in the future, both on your own account and in terms of the confidence you have in those around you. You needn't take no for an answer with regard to issues you see as being crucial to your ultimate success, and can afford to put colleagues right if you think their ideas are barmy.

8 SATURDAY
Moon Age Day 29   Moon Sign Scorpio

For three days in a row the Moon has been in Scorpio, and although it is losing power now you can still utilise the boost it has given you in order to enjoy Saturday. Now less inclined to think about practical and professional matters, you have scope to have fun, and should have no difficulty enlisting allies.

9 SUNDAY
Moon Age Day 0   Moon Sign Sagittarius

This would be a very good time to develop your personal resources and to look towards home-based matters in greater detail. Even if you are more inclined to stay at home than was the case yesterday, you can still find plenty to keep you occupied and it is very unlikely you will be bored.

10 MONDAY   *Moon Age Day 1   Moon Sign Sagittarius*

This is another good period during which to get started with financial projects and initiatives. Mercury is in your solar second house, suggesting you should have no difficulty whatsoever in getting your message across, whatever it is. Beware of getting too tied down with pointless red tape or mindless tasks.

11 TUESDAY   *Moon Age Day 2   Moon Sign Capricorn*

Your initiative and thinking power remain well starred, and you should know exactly what you want from any given situation, even if others flounder somewhat. You can't expect everyone to keep up with your quick thinking and there are probably going to be times now when you will have to go it alone.

12 WEDNESDAY   *Moon Age Day 3   Moon Sign Capricorn*

You are entering a fairly protracted period during which you can ensure that your financial state is slightly better. That's saying something with Christmas just around the corner, but is partly because you are so good at getting a bargain almost everywhere you look. At the same time you may decide to repay debts from the past.

13 THURSDAY   *Moon Age Day 4   Moon Sign Capricorn*

This is a day during which you would be wise to avoid getting on the wrong side of others. The fact is that not everyone may be equally easy to either read or to approach. If colleagues especially seem particularly grumpy, this might be a good day to leave them alone. You can approach them better by early next week.

14 FRIDAY   *Moon Age Day 5   Moon Sign Aquarius*

Under current influences, financial opportunities and your money sense remain highlighted, and you may find that you are now in a position to command a better salary. Personal incentives are also well accented, and this would be an ideal day to approach a prospective romantic partner.

15 SATURDAY
Moon Age Day 6   Moon Sign Aquarius

You cannot afford to remain quiet or to lock yourself away this weekend. Your interests are best served by being out and about, enjoying what life has to offer and also learning more that will be to your own advantage eventually. Rules and regulations can get on your nerves once again, especially if they threaten to mar your weekend.

16 SUNDAY
Moon Age Day 7   Moon Sign Pisces

Any Scorpio people who have been rather uptight recently now have scope to loosen up and to express their desires in a better way. You can afford to take time out to be with loved ones and to keep an open attitude to all issues. There are some strange attitudes around, but make sure yours is not one of them!

17 MONDAY
Moon Age Day 8   Moon Sign Pisces

Practical affairs have a great deal going for them now, and in terms of money you have potential to make progress. Be prepared to look for genuine bargains as far as those last-minute purchases are concerned, even if that means waiting until even closer to Christmas to get what you are looking for.

18 TUESDAY
Moon Age Day 9   Moon Sign Aries

There could be even further gains to be made in the financial sphere, thanks to the present position of the Sun in your solar second house. However, it only stays there for three or four days longer and after that, there's a danger you may decide to spend lavishly. You can find new ways to enjoy yourself tonight.

19 WEDNESDAY
Moon Age Day 10   Moon Sign Aries

In your professional and work life you need to be ready to explore new ground, even though Christmas is just around the corner. You can make gains whilst others have taken their eye off the ball, and this is going to be important in the New Year. In a romantic sense you have scope to act on impulse now.

20 THURSDAY   *Moon Age Day 11   Moon Sign Taurus*

Even if you feel less in charge of your life for the next couple of days, at least you will get the lunar low out of the way before Christmas comes along. Don't be surprised if the last thing you want to do is to go out and have a good time socially. Many Scorpios might simply opt for a warm fire and a good book.

21 FRIDAY   *Moon Age Day 12   Moon Sign Taurus*

This is a low-key planetary phase and so you may decide that pushing yourself is just a waste of time. What you can do is to look and plan ahead. Your mind remains razor-sharp, and there is little to prevent you from putting matters in hand for projects you know cannot mature for several weeks or even months.

22 SATURDAY   *Moon Age Day 13   Moon Sign Gemini*

This is a very favourable time for investigations of almost any sort. All the more reason to get your detective head on, as almost anything mysterious could really captivate your attention. Don't be too quick to judge others, especially regarding issues you are not entirely sure about yourself.

23 SUNDAY   *Moon Age Day 14   Moon Sign Gemini*

Now your mental abilities and your powers of communication are reaching a potential peak. It would take a very good person to fool you in any way and the fact is that you can see through situations as if they were made of glass. New creative pursuits could be on your mind, and these may slightly overtake you.

24 MONDAY   *Moon Age Day 15   Moon Sign Cancer*

You have scope to make everyday routines a little more interesting and even exciting, though with Christmas only a day away you might be frustrated in some of your practical efforts. Instead of worrying about such things, it would be sensible to simply pitch in and have a good time with your family and friends.

25 TUESDAY   *Moon Age Day 16   Moon Sign Cancer*

You can bring folk round to your way of thinking on this Christmas Day, and you are wonderful at defusing any difficult situation. You can make sure the floor is yours and that everyone wants to listen to what you have to say. Getting to grips with a past family matter might seem a strange way to spend today, but it's certainly an option!

26 WEDNESDAY   *Moon Age Day 17   Moon Sign Leo*

Differences of opinion are possible today, maybe over what you want to do in a social sense. You need to compromise and will have a better time if you are willing to do so. You may decide to travel a short way in order to see someone who lives at a distance or who is rarely at home.

27 THURSDAY   *Moon Age Day 18   Moon Sign Leo*

There is plenty of scope about in terms of new attachments, and even existing relationships are strengthened by present planetary trends. Don't be too quick to apportion blame if something goes slightly wrong. A better response is to pitch in and sort matters out yourself.

28 FRIDAY   *Moon Age Day 19   Moon Sign Leo*

Personal rewards are achievable as a result of your generosity of spirit, which is extremely high at the moment. Mercury gives you even better powers of communication and assists you to form a bridge with someone you haven't always got on well with in the past. You may already be formulating New Year's resolutions, but take it steady!

29 SATURDAY   *Moon Age Day 20   Moon Sign Virgo*

You can make this a busy but nonetheless inspiring time. Whether or not you are actually back at work, you should find plenty to keep you occupied and no lack of incentive when it comes to showing yourself off in social situations. You can persuade everyone to be your friend.

30 SUNDAY   *Moon Age Day 21   Moon Sign Virgo*

Even if you are quite willing to make sacrifices for the sake of friends, beware of letting anyone take advantage of your good nature. This should not be too much of a problem if you are on the ball today and don't allow yourself to be used. Romance looks especially rewarding under present trends.

31 MONDAY   *Moon Age Day 22   Moon Sign Libra*

Attracting the good things in life should be no problem today and you can afford to look ahead towards the New Year in a very progressive manner. It's worth keeping abreast of changes to plans, especially those that mean long-distance travel in a few months. Also stand by for a potentially romantic end to the year.

RISING SIGNS FOR SCORPIO

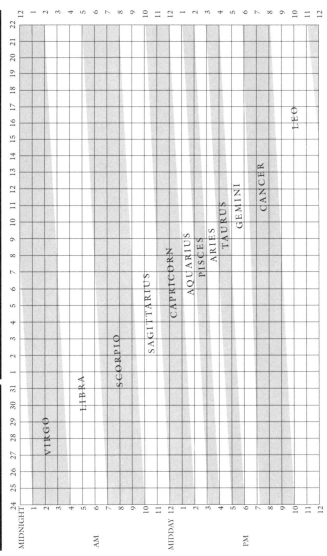

THE ZODIAC, PLANETS AND CORRESPONDENCES

The Earth revolves around the Sun once every calendar year, so when viewed from Earth the Sun appears in a different part of the sky as the year progresses. In astrology, these parts of the sky are divided into the signs of the zodiac and this means that the signs are organised in a circle. The circle begins with Aries and ends with Pisces.

Taking the zodiac sign as a starting point, astrologers then work with all the positions of planets, stars and many other factors to calculate horoscopes and birth charts and tell us what the stars have in store for us.

The table below shows the planets and Elements for each of the signs of the zodiac. Each sign belongs to one of the four Elements: Fire, Air, Earth or Water. Fire signs are creative and enthusiastic; Air signs are mentally active and thoughtful; Earth signs are constructive and practical; Water signs are emotional and have strong feelings.

It also shows the metals and gemstones associated with, or corresponding with, each sign. The correspondence is made when a metal or stone possesses properties that are held in common with a particular sign of the zodiac.

Finally, the table shows the opposite of each star sign – this is the opposite sign in the astrological circle.

Placed	Sign	Symbol	Element	Planet	Metal	Stone	Opposite
1	Aries	Ram	Fire	Mars	Iron	Bloodstone	Libra
2	Taurus	Bull	Earth	Venus	Copper	Sapphire	Scorpio
3	Gemini	Twins	Air	Mercury	Mercury	Tiger's Eye	Sagittarius
4	Cancer	Crab	Water	Moon	Silver	Pearl	Capricorn
5	Leo	Lion	Fire	Sun	Gold	Ruby	Aquarius
6	Virgo	Maiden	Earth	Mercury	Mercury	Sardonyx	Pisces
7	Libra	Scales	Air	Venus	Copper	Sapphire	Aries
8	Scorpio	Scorpion	Water	Pluto	Plutonium	Jasper	Taurus
9	Sagittarius	Archer	Fire	Jupiter	Tin	Topaz	Gemini
10	Capricorn	Goat	Earth	Saturn	Lead	Black Onyx	Cancer
11	Aquarius	Waterbearer	Air	Uranus	Uranium	Amethyst	Leo
12	Pisces	Fishes	Water	Neptune	Tin	Moonstone	Virgo